When his daughter, Darcy, stepped out of the fitting room, he felt his heart catch.

She looked adorable. The pink top was perfect. The jeans made her look taller than he'd expected. It wouldn't be too long before she grew up completely. For a moment he was shaken that he'd almost missed all this. Anger against his ex burned. She should have told him he had a daughter.

When Maddie stepped out of the dressing room, Ty stared at her. She looked just like her country twin sister—in jeans and a yellow shirt. If he didn't know better, he'd think she was a cowgirl.

"You look like your sister now," Darcy said, unconsciously echoing Ty's thoughts.

"I always look like her. We're twins," she said.

"Looks can be deceiving," Ty said.

Maddie eyed him. "Or not. I may not be a cowgirl from way back, but I can learn."

* * *

Books by Barbara McMahon

Love Inspired

The Family Next Door
Rocky Point Reunion
Rocky Point Promise
Mirror Image Bride

BARBARA McMAHON

was born and raised in the southern U.S., but settled in California after spending a year flying around the world for an international airline. She settled down to raise a family and work for a computer firm, and began writing when her children started school. Now, feeling fortunate to have been able to realize a long-held dream of quitting her day job and writing full-time, she and her husband have moved to the Sierra Nevada of California, where she finds her desire to write is stronger than ever. With the beauty of the mountains visible from her windows, and the pace of life slower than that of the hectic San Francisco Bay Area, where they previously resided, she finds more time than ever to think up stories and characters and share them with others through writing.

Barbara loves to hear from readers. You can reach her at P.O. Box 977, Pioneer, CA 95666-0977, U.S.A. Readers can also contact Barbara at her website, www.barbaramcmahon.com.

Mirror Image Bride

Barbara McMahon

Love Inspired

Special thanks and acknowledgment to Barbara McMahon for her participation in the Texas Twins miniseries.

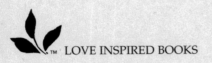 LOVE INSPIRED BOOKS

Recycling programs for this product may not exist in your area.

ISBN-13: 978-0-373-08246-9

MIRROR IMAGE BRIDE

www.LoveInspiredBooks.com

Printed in U.S.A.

Be on your guard; stand firm in the faith;
be men of courage; be strong.
—*1 Corinthians* 16:13

To Bridgette: Do you still miss Texas?
Love always.

Chapter One

Maddie Wallace stepped out into the early morning west Texas sunshine and drew a deep breath. Quietly closing the door behind her, she smiled in anticipation at the beautiful day. Not a cloud in the sky. She drew another breath and wrinkled her nose. While the air was fresh and clean compared to Fort Worth's city fumes, it smelled of fresh hay, a hint of sage and lots of cattle. Did anyone get used to that smell if they lived here long enough?

She walked down the flagstone pathway that led through the iron gates and headed for the foreman's house—only a three-minute walk from the sprawling brick home she'd been staying in for almost a month. Today was the first day of her new job. Wiping her palms on the sides of her dark slacks, she had a moment of apprehension. She wasn't really a nanny. What if she was a total flop? Desperate times called for desperate measures and when the offer came, however reluctantly, she'd jumped at it. She was not one to freeload.

Not that her newly discovered twin ever hinted at such a thing. She'd suggested this opportunity with Ty as a way to keep Maddie in Grasslands.

"It's the perfect answer," Violet had said yesterday after they happened upon Ty and his daughter, Darcy, looking after a sow and her babies in one of the small barns. "You'd be helping Ty, and it means you'd stay here for a while longer at least. I'm not ready to lose my sister yet."

"I'm in," Maddie'd said to the sister she hadn't even known existed a month ago. "But it's possible Ty doesn't want me."

When the twins both turned to Ty, the handsome cowboy seemed genuinely torn. "I guess we could give it a test run," he had finally conceded after a long pause. "Maybe until school starts, anyway."

Although the sisters breathed a collective sigh of relief, Maddie still harbored secret doubts about sticking around. After all, to discover at age twenty-five that she had a twin sister was almost more than she could take in. Who would have suspected that breaking up with her fiancé would result in finding a part of her family she never knew about?

Once again a thousand questions flooded her mind. What had happened so long ago to split their family? Why had her father never mentioned he had other children? Why let her and her brothers believe the only mother they'd ever known was their real mother when it seemed apparent now that Belle Colby was her mother? Hers and her older brother Grayson's.

Everything had been topsy-turvy in the past month. This job offer, such as it was, added to the Alice-down-the-rabbit-hole feeling.

But she was willing to give it a shot—especially after seeing the way Ty had kept a watchful eye over his little girl when she ran out of the barn and began scampering around the property. It filled Maddie with relief to see Darcy momentarily escaping the reality of losing her mother and moving someplace new. She could only imagine what a shock it must have been for the poor child to arrive at the ranch from Houston without a clue the man she met for the first time was her father.

As Darcy chased the goat around, Jack's dog, Nipper, barked at their antics, which had Darcy dissolving into gales of laughter. For a few precious minutes, she was a happy little girl. Yet, despite the girl's burst of exuberance, Maddie was struck by the bleak expression in Ty's eyes.

"Really, I'll do a good job," she said earnestly, trying to reassure him. "I mean, I can cook breakfast for her—I know you get up early and are already at work when most of us are just getting up."

"City slickers," he murmured, but thankfully didn't rescind the job offer.

Granted, the job wasn't ideal, but it enabled her to stay on the ranch and get to know her sister and brother better.

Snapping back to reality, Maddie glanced at the corral where several horses stood, ears pricked, awaiting their morning hay. It was still amazing to her that she was here on the Colby Ranch.

What if she had not responded to Landon's phone call a month ago? She'd been avoiding him ever since she'd broken their engagement. Yet answering had led her to discovering she had an identical twin she hadn't known about. She had invited Violet to her apartment that fateful afternoon. Once inside, her twin had been drawn to some of the photographs on the mantel—especially a favorite one of her father and two brothers. Violet had been startled to see Grayson—a twin to her brother Jack!

Violet had invited her to the ranch, and Maddie had agreed. With her father away on a missionary trip due to last until Thanksgiving, and her two brothers unavailable, it seemed the perfect time to go. Landon thought she was rushing into something that required a bit more contemplation, but she'd gone with her instincts.

It still seemed weird to look at Violet and

see herself. As far as they could piece together, they'd been separated as babies, each parent taking one of each of the two sets of twins. Jack had been kept in the dark, just like her—and he hadn't taken the news well.

Even their longtime housekeeper, Rachel Everett, had not known the truth when Maddie called her to tell her about Violet and where she'd be going for a few weeks.

Now they were all asking the same question—what had happened to their family so long ago?

Reaching the small porch in front of Ty Garland's wooden house, she stepped onto it, her shoes echoing on the surface. The small house was rather plain with a porch that ran the width of it, green shutters flanking the two windows, and a green door in the center. While the clapboard was white, the mossy green was the same color used on the barn trim. Her focus shifted to the job at hand. She hadn't felt this nervous since her first day on the job at *Texas Today,* the beloved magazine she'd worked on for three years. Budget cuts had eliminated her job. She'd been devastated at the time.

Now, losing her job seemed like the work of God. She'd had time to extend her visit and a job had materialized almost the same moment she began to talk about returning to Fort Worth.

Thank You, Lord, for working this all out. Please, let us find some answers soon. And please let me do a good job here.

Ty Garland was the foreman of Colby Ranch. A week ago, to his stunned amazement, he'd found out he had a daughter—an eight-year-old little girl who was coming to live with him. According to Violet the news had rocked him. He hadn't even known his ex-wife had had a child, much less that it was his.

The foreman's job came with a small house, situated between the large brick house the Colbys lived in and the huge barn that held horses, hay and other accoutrements needed for ranching. She'd been given a tour of the prosperous ranch when she'd first arrived.

This past month had given her a chance to get to know Violet and, to a lesser degree, Jack.

She was so delighted to have her twin sister in her life. She should focus on her blessings and live in the here and now. Speaking of which, she'd signed on to watch the little girl so in need of help and hoped she could do a good job. Ty's displeasure was not something she wanted. Quietly, she said a quick prayer for wisdom and guidance in dealing with Darcy. And her dad.

Knocking on the front door, she waited. Turning, she surveyed the barnyard, which was coming awake as the sun rose. Chickens searched for food in the dirt around the corral. Three horses remained standing near the fence. She could hear the nanny goat bleating. Was she waiting for food, too?

It was still, quiet and pleasant. Quite a difference from her rented high-rise condo in Fort Worth on a busy thoroughfare. Unexpectedly, she was growing used to it. Growing to appreciate the silence of the early morning. The beauty of God's handiwork spread before her. The ageless work of cowboys raising beef for the masses.

Ty opened the door and she turned, a bright smile on her face.

"Good morning. Here as promised." She was good at pretending she didn't feel as nervous as she did.

Maddie held her smile even though he merely nodded and opened the door wider for her to enter. The tall, fit cowboy with the stern face gave a whole new meaning to the word *taciturn*. He topped her by several inches. Without his hat, his dark hair gleamed in the light. His dark eyes rarely gave anything away. She always felt small and feminine around his wide shoulders, strong arms.

She'd met him several weeks ago when she'd first come to the Colby Ranch. Over the days since, she'd seen him often enough when he discussed ranch business with Violet and Jack. Yet she didn't feel she knew him any better today than that first day. Not for lack of trying. She always had a greeting for him when they met. He usually touched the edge of his cowboy hat with two fingers and moved on.

His frowning eyes met hers. She knew in a heartbeat he thought this was a dumb idea. Her gaze locked with his and Maddie wondered if Ty had only agreed to the arrangement because his boss put him on the spot. Now Maddie was having second thoughts herself. Could she work for this man? He was unlike anyone else she knew. Usually people were friendly enough when she smiled at them.

Not Ty. He replied to any direct questions with as few words as possible. Still, she was glad for the job opportunity. She'd been out of work for six weeks and her savings would only stretch so far.

The assignment was simple enough—watch Ty's daughter for a month or so until he could make other arrangements. But could she deal with being in constant contact with the man whom she'd steered clear of in the weeks she'd been on the ranch? He obviously didn't like her.

Much as she wanted to dislike him, she

didn't. He fascinated her. He looked as at home on a horse as he did walking. He'd study the day as others might study a financial report. She often wondered what he saw when he gazed off in the distance. His air of quiet confidence made the other ranch hands look brash and wild. His manner was always respectful, but distant. She had yet to see him smile and sometimes at night she'd daydream various ways to get him to smile. So far no brilliant ideas had come forth.

"We're in the kitchen," he said, heading down a short hall toward the back of the house. Maddie quickly followed, glancing into the living room as they walked by. A big recliner sat against one wall, lined up perfectly with the big flat-screen TV that hung on the opposite wall. There was a comfortable leather sofa with a throw over one arm. The coffee table was scarred as if he'd put his feet on it many times. There were beverage stains and a stack of what looked like ranching journals and a day-old newspaper. The hardwood floors rang with the sound of her shoes.

Stepping into the kitchen, she smiled at Ty's eight-year-old daughter.

Maddie liked the kitchen the instant she stepped in. The wide window over the sink framed a beautiful view of the land as it spread out in front of her. Trees scattered here and there, a slight roll to the ground. In the distance she could see some of the cattle grazing.

The appliances were fairly new and were in pristine shape. No dishes in the sink, nothing on the counter but a toaster and coffee machine. Ty kept a neat home.

Maddie was glad the job required her to cook for this small family. It meant she wouldn't have to share a dining room with Violet and Landon when he came to visit. After all, the newly engaged couple deserved their privacy.

"Good morning," she said. "Ready for breakfast?"

"I guess," Darcy said, darting a quick glance at her father.

Maddie looked at Ty also, struck by the

mixture of confusion, hurt and longing she saw there. Her heart went out to him.

Maddie knew exactly how both Darcy and Ty felt. She had not known about her sister, he had not known about his daughter. Why did people do that? Keep families apart? It hurt to know her mother had so easily walked away and that her dad had never mentioned his other two children.

Pushing away the thoughts that spun in her mind daily, she focused on Darcy. Was it any more difficult to find the father she'd been told was dead was alive and had never known she existed?

Maddie hoped the little girl would bounce back faster than she was doing with the stunning news about her own family. Darcy had lost her mother only a week and a half ago when a drunk driver had rammed her car. Her grandparents were out of the country and no one had reached them yet. She wound up on the doorstep of a father who had never known she'd been born. How confusing and scary was that?

Ty looked at her. "We'll try this for a couple

of days. If you can't hack it, I'll find someone else."

"I'll do my best," she said, hoping he would
genuinely give her a chance and not merely
bide his time until he could fire her. "What's
your favorite breakfast?" she asked the little
girl, hoping she could do something to ease
the pain of loss and set this child on the right
path to recovering from her grief.

"Pancakes," Darcy said, her forlorn expression tugging at Maddie's heartstrings.

"One stack of hotcakes coming up."

Ty poured himself a mug of coffee and gestured to the machine, which Maddie took as
an invitation to help herself. She nodded and
then took a few minutes getting familiar with
Ty's kitchen. She felt his eyes on her the entire time. Gathering all the ingredients, she
enlisted Darcy's help as they prepared the bat-
ter. Soon golden pancakes were filling plates.
Ty had rocked back on the chair he sat on and
balanced on the back two legs, watching her
without saying a word.

Once or twice Darcy had glanced his way,
halfway curious, halfway uncertain.

"All ready," Maddie said, placing another golden pancake on a stack she kept warm in the oven.

Ty's chair came down with a thump that startled her.

She looked at him. His dark eyes stared back into hers, then he nodded.

If that was the best he could do, she'd take it.

"What do you want us to do today?" she asked him.

"You're in charge of her," he said, eating the pancakes, taking a sip of the hot coffee.

"Can I see the horses?" Darcy asked.

"Sure. We'll go to the barn when we finish eating." Maddie made the suggestion but watched Ty to make sure he was okay with that.

As the silence dragged, Maddie began to get annoyed. "We need to talk about this job," she said.

He looked at her. "What about it?"

"I need to know what you expect, what my duties will entail. I have never done this before."

He looked exasperated. "That much was obvious when Violet first suggested the arrangement. Mainly watch Darcy—keep her safe and give her something to do."

"And fix the meals."

He quirked a brow. "That a problem?"

"No. Not at all. I like to cook. I imagine you like plain food."

"As compared to what?" he asked, watching her warily.

"Cordon bleu."

"Can you cook like that?"

She grinned and shook her head. "No, but I can make some fancy stuff."

Darcy watched the exchange with wide eyes.

"Plain wholesome foods and plenty of it," he said.

"Ummm. Do you ever cook out back?" She'd caught a glimpse of a grill when she'd passed the window over the sink a few minutes ago.

"Most of the summer that's what I do if I don't eat with the men—steaks, mostly."

Figured, working on a cattle ranch.

Once the meal was finished, Ty surprised Maddie by clearing his dish and cup, putting them in the sink.

He lifted his cowboy hat off a peg and plopped it on. He walked toward the back door. "I have chores to do." He opened the door and turned to look at her. "Tell Violet if you need anything. She knows how to reach me on the range."

Maddie swallowed hard and nodded. He intimidated her. There were no two ways about it. But his daughter was adorable. Her straight brown hair framed a heart-shaped face. Her dark brown eyes watched Maddie with a somber expression. She looked confused and unhappy and sad. Her mother had just died. That was a hard thing to deal with at any age.

Hadn't her own mother—the woman she'd always thought of as her mother—died suddenly when Maddie had been a few years younger than Darcy? It had been a solo car accident, the vehicle spinning out of control on a rain-slicked street.

For a moment, Maddie remembered her lost, confused and sad self at age five. If she hadn't had her brothers she didn't know what she would have done. Darcy had no one.

Ty looked at Darcy. "Mind Maddie, hear?"

She nodded solemnly.

The door closed and Maddie looked at Darcy. Memories of her own mother, of her loss so many years ago, had been at the forefront these last few weeks. Nothing anyone could say would bring her mother back, nor Darcy's. It was up to them to move forward, as hard as that was. She smiled gently at the little girl.

"I'll do the dishes while you get dressed, then we can head for the barn."

"Okay." Darcy dashed down the hall.

Running water in the sink, Maddie thought about Ty and how hard it must have been to suddenly discover he had a daughter.

"His wife should have told him," Maddie murmured to herself. From what Violet had said, if Darcy's grandparents hadn't been out of touch it was doubtful the state would have even looked for Ty.

It was a big thing to have a parent one never knew about. Maddie gazed out the window, feeling the loss anew of her mother. To discover that Sharla Wallace hadn't been her biological mother still stunned her. Closing her eyes, for a second she could almost feel her loving touch. Feel the love that always enveloped her when her mom hugged her or rocked her in that big rocking chair. It had been twenty years since she'd felt her loving hands, heard her laughter, listened to her stories of when she'd been a little girl.

Now she'd learned Belle Colby was her mother, her biological mother.

She still had difficulty absorbing that. Maybe it would be easier if Belle was at the ranch and could offer an explanation for so many of the questions she had. In a wry twist of fate, only a few days before Violet had shown up in Fort Worth and set the entire course of events in motion, Belle had been thrown from a horse and suffered a traumatic brain injury. She was still in a coma six weeks later.

"I'm ready," Darcy said, coming back into the kitchen wearing pink shorts and a pink-and-white shirt. Tennis shoes on her feet.

Maddie turned to smile at her. "And faster than I got these dishes done."

Thinking about things would have to wait. She had a little girl to take care of.

Ty finished giving the men their assignments for the day and went to saddle his own horse. For the first time since he'd heard about Darcy, he felt he could make it through the day. The stunned knowledge, the overwhelming feeling of inadequacy, was held at bay. He had Maddie now to watch her. Maybe she could relate to Darcy. He sure hadn't been able to.

Once the horse was ready, he mounted and headed out of the barn and into the bright Texas sun. He was going to ride the fence line at the far boundary. One of the hands had spotted Colby cattle on the neighbor's property and wondered if there was a breach in the fence. Instead of assigning that cowboy to find out, Ty decided to ride out himself. He needed the time away from the insurmountable problems in the homestead. Time to try to wrap his head around the fact that a week ago he hadn't even known he had an eight-year-old daughter.

One week since the social services woman had called. A week to accept his ex-wife, Brittany, had deceived him in more ways than one. A week to get used to having a daughter—and having her show up to live with him.

As he rode, the routine of his job took hold. He loved being out on the range, loved the peace and serenity that came from being only him and his horse. Gradually some of the stress and tension began to ease. At least he could ride away today. The last five days he'd been so preoccupied with Darcy that his mind hadn't been on the job.

Not that he regretted a moment of that time. She was a wonder. Although she resembled her mother in many ways, she had inherited his brown hair and dark eyes. He couldn't help wondering if they shared other traits as well. He didn't know if she was naturally shy, or only around him, but he was doing his best to make her feel at ease.

And doing a bad job, he knew.

But he wasn't used to children. He hadn't

a clue what made them tick. And especially not a girl raised in the city, used to the lifestyle his ex-wife had embraced with fervor once their marriage ended.

Anger at Brittany boiled over again. He looked up at the sky, silently asking how she could have hated him so much to keep all knowledge of his only daughter from him.

An only, spoiled child, Brittany had been impossible to live with when she didn't get her way. Things went from bad to worse when he broke his leg in the rodeo and he was out. She balked when he told her that his rodeo days were over and he wanted to settle on a ranch. Brittany had tried to convince him to take a cushy job in Houston working for his father, but he told her he wasn't cut out for the corporate world. He'd known she was angry, but he had no clue how much she resented him—or how far-reaching the emotional fallout would be.

Brittany stayed with him while he recovered, but made her position clear—ranch life wasn't for her. Two months later, he was served with divorce papers. Judging by

Darcy's birthday, Brittany had to have known she was pregnant. Once he was fit enough to ride, he kept his head held high and found a spot at the Colby ranch. He moved forward with his plans, but never in his wildest dreams would he have fathomed that he had a daughter out there somewhere.

Ty gripped the reins tighter in the futility of trying to understand how a woman he'd once loved, who had declared she loved him, could have behaved so underhandedly and cruelly.

"Lord, if You're listening, I could use some help here. I don't know what the future's going to hold, but I'm hoping Darcy and I can build a bond that nothing will break. That I'll be a better father to her than mine was to me. Don't let me mess this up, please, Lord."

He had to believe there was some hope on the horizon. Two years ago he was promoted to foreman at the Colby ranch. It was the closest thing he had to owning his own ranch until he could make that dream a reality.

Ty had been as surprised as Jack Colby when Violet returned from Fort Worth with an identical twin. He hadn't heard much about the situation. That was a Colby family matter and deserved privacy. But once or twice Jack had said something. Apparently, he had a twin out there somewhere as well.

When Violet had suggested yesterday that Maddie watch Darcy for a few weeks, he'd been dumfounded. And against the idea entirely.

Maddie Wallace was from Fort Worth. Bright lights, a thriving nightlife and lots of cultural stimulation for a sophisticated career woman. Maddie wouldn't last a month as nanny to his daughter. She'd be like Brittany, feeling constrained on the ranch, bored, anxious for the excitement cities offered and were definitely missing from a working ranch.

He only needed a month. In September, Darcy started school. He'd see if he could find a mom in town who would babysit after school until he could pick her up. Until next summer. Who knew what would happen by then? Maybe Josh, one of the ranch cowboys, would get married to that gal he was courting and Ty would have someone on the ranch to watch Darcy. That part he'd trust to the Lord.

He reached the fence and began patrolling. Until he found a break, there was nothing keeping his thoughts from straying to his new nanny. He envisioned her plain as day. She looked like Violet, yet didn't. They were identical, yet her features were a tiny bit sharper. Her auburn hair brushed her shoulders, looking soft in the sunlight, with gold strands gleaming in the sun. Her brown eyes, which she often covered with sunglasses, looked like melted chocolate. The lashes were dark and thick.

Ty scowled. He had no business comparing any woman's eyes with chocolate. He had to figure if he should be looking for a local woman who could watch Darcy. Someone used to ranch life, instead of someone city bred and as out of place on the ranch as the Queen of England.

Maybe that was the reason Violet suggested Maddie. She lived the same kind of life Darcy had. They'd relate. And both were like fish out of water. Maddie had been here almost a month and still wore silk blouses and open-toed shoes. Even Brittany had known better.

Maddie reminded him of Brittany. He knew it was unfair to judge a person on outward appearances, but he couldn't help it. She was gloss and glamour, and he needed someone practical and down to earth. He didn't believe it was going to work.

Of course the next one to watch Darcy wouldn't be as pretty, he knew. Probably wouldn't have that constant cheerful smile that had him taking a second look. And a third. He wasn't sure what she had to smile about. She'd lost her job, found out she'd been lied to her entire life and was now temporarily hired to be a nanny. And apparently, she was alone in the world except for the Colbys as her own brothers were away and her father was not responding to her calls.

Note to the future—he'd be there for his daughter when she needed him.

Once the kitchen was spotless, Maddie and Darcy went to the barn. The horses fascinated the little girl, and Maddie was trying to get used to them. She envied Violet's lack of trepidation when around the large animals. Together, Maddie and Darcy walked through the wide center portion, looking at the empty stalls, studying the hay stacked in the loft high overhead, wondering how the bales had made it up there. Most of the horses were either being ridden by the cowboys or were in the corral at the side of the barn.

As Maddie watched the little girl dart here and there, she wondered if she would be up to the task. A local woman would have been a better choice, someone who already knew about the ranches, about cattle, horses and cowboys. This child would soon find out all she needed as she grew up on the ranch from someone like that.

Maddie, on the other hand, believed she'd always feel awkward and out of step. It seemed to be a lifestyle one needed to be raised in to fully understand. She'd never even visited a dude ranch, much less a working ranch. And much as she loved being with her sister, learning more about her life and coming face-to-face with identical likes and dislikes, she also felt in the way.

Especially since Violet and Landon had fallen in love.

Talk about a curveball! Only two months ago Landon had been pressuring her for a wedding date. Now he was head over heels in love with her twin. Not that Maddie wanted to marry him, as she'd explained when she'd broken their engagement. He hadn't taken no for an answer at first, claiming she was having premarital jitters. But their relationship had never felt totally right. He'd been a friend whom she'd dated for months. When he proposed, she accepted, hoping her feelings would strengthen to be what she thought a wife should feel for a husband.

What did she know? Her mother had died when she'd been five. Her father had never remarried. So she only saw married couples from a distance. Their widowed housekeeper, Rachel, had raised her and her brothers. Still, she was never able to envision herself living with Landon. She'd somehow known from the beginning the two of them wouldn't make it.

He was a great guy, and she was delighted he'd found his true love with Violet.

Maddie once again pushed away the thought of Belle Colby. She had had weeks to get used to the idea that the woman was her mother. Yet the only interaction they'd had was when Maddie went to visit her with Violet. Despite Belle's grim prognosis, Violet remained hopeful for recovery. Maddie spoke to her, prayed with her sister for her healing, but still she felt nothing of Belle to connect her as her mother.

She'd seen photographs of Belle with Violet and Jack from when they'd been little. There was no doubt they were her children, which had to mean she and Grayson were also her children. But the instant rapport she'd yearned for wasn't there. Not as it had been with Violet.

"Can we ride a horse?" Darcy asked, interrupting her ruminations.

"We can ask your dad. I'm sure he'll want you to learn to ride."

"Then I could ride everywhere," Darcy said, coming to stand beside Maddie. "Can you ride?"

"Not very well."

"Maybe he can teach you, too," she said, heading out of the barn.

Maddie smiled at that suggestion. She doubted Ty wanted to spend a minute more with her than he had to. But she had enough questions to ask him when he got home.

She smiled in anticipation. It would give her another reason to spend a bit more time with Ty—and the confusing feelings she had for him. She could hardly wait.

Chapter Two

By lunchtime, Maddie was glad to leave the barn area and return to Ty's air-conditioned house.

"Thank You, Lord, for this," she murmured as she and Darcy entered.

"What?" Darcy asked, looking up at her.

"I'm giving a thanks prayer to the Lord for the coolness," she said.

"Oh." Darcy was quiet for a moment, then asked, "Can you ask God why my mommy died?"

"Honey, it was a terrible accident." Maddie gave her a quick hug.

From what she'd learned from Violet, the drunk driver had come from a side street and T-boned the driver's side of Brittany Parker's car, killing her instantly. Maddie was thankful Darcy had not been in the car.

She released Darcy with a pat on her shoulder. "You're with your dad now, he'll take good care of you."

"Mommy said my dad was dead."

"He wasn't. He's been here all along, waiting for you to come live with him," Maddie said, wondering how to explain things to the child when she herself didn't understand his ex-wife's behavior.

"Why didn't he ever come visit me? Especially at Christmas. My grandmama and grandpa always come to visit at Christmas. It's time for family."

"He didn't know where you lived."

Darcy considered that for a moment, then shrugged. "I don't like it here. When can I go home?"

"This is your home now," Maddie said as they headed for the kitchen.

"No, it's not. I live at 2733 Aspen Street, Houston, Texas."

"That's the home you had with your mom. Now you live here with your dad." Maddie switched gears to try to lift the girl's mood. "Let's eat lunch and we can talk about what you want to do this afternoon."

"Are you going to spend the afternoon with me?"

"I am. In fact, I'm going to be watching you during the day while your dad's working. How's that?"

Darcy shrugged, pulling her mouth down. "Okay, I guess."

What a ringing endorsement, Maddie thought, but tried not to feel discouraged.

She glanced through the wide window over the sink when she stepped into the kitchen. She loved the beautiful view.

"What would you like for lunch?" Maddie asked, rummaging around, looking for bread and dishes.

"Peanut butter and grape jam. He bought some grape jam for me 'cause I like it."

"He?" Maddie asked.

"You know, my dad," Darcy said in a quiet voice.

Maddie wondered what Darcy was thinking. So far she hadn't heard the child refer to Ty as anything but "he."

Darcy sat at the big, farm-style table, kicking the legs of the chair as she watched Maddie open cupboard doors and look into the refrigerator. By the time Maddie had found all she needed, Darcy had regained her more chatty nature. She talked about the pigs and the chickens and the goat and the fact Violet grew vegetables. That seemed to fascinate her. To Darcy, produce came from the grocery store, not the ground.

"When we finish eating we'll check out supplies and plan on what to have for supper," Maddie said, finding the silverware drawer.

"Are you going to cook our supper?" Darcy asked.

"I am. And breakfast in the morning."

"*He* gets up very early," Darcy said.

"Hmmm, maybe you and I don't need to get up that early. Shall we ask? I mean, it's not like we have to get riding before it gets hot or have hours of work in front of us."

She needed to talk to Ty to see what he expected. Maybe he'd want her there for breakfast each morning. Getting up early wasn't her favorite thing to do, but it would be worth it to see Ty first thing each morning. Was his attitude softening toward her? She considered it might be wishful thinking, but she was holding on to the thought.

Once she knew what he expected, she could make plans accordingly. Maddie's boss had always said she was an expert at that.

Her former boss, she amended silently, feeling a pang that she wasn't in Fort Worth, working frantically to get the next edition of *Texas Today* to bed. She missed the hectic atmosphere, the camaraderie of her coworkers. The sense of accomplishment when the issue was finally on its way to the stands.

Sighing, she cut their sandwiches, poured milk and sat to eat. Another change in her topsy-turvy world.

"What are we going to do this afternoon?" Darcy asked as she was finishing her sandwich.

"How about some artwork? Did you bring any coloring books or crayons to color with?"

Darcy shook her head. "The lady who

came to tell my babysitter my mom was dead packed clothes and left everything else at our apartment. And she didn't even pack my favorite dress."

"No toys or books or anything?"

"I got to bring Teddy bear, that's all," Darcy said, kicking the legs of her chair again.

Maddie had no idea how social services worked. Surely at some point the apartment had to be vacated for the next tenant. What would happen to all of Darcy's things? And those of her mother? Surely they'd come to Darcy.

Another item to discuss with Ty.

Once they'd finished lunch, they walked over to the main house. The large, warm, brick home easily housed the Colby family and any guests they wanted. Maddie still felt a bit like an interloper when she entered without knocking. This was the home her sister and brother lived in. A far cry from the modest house she'd been raised in. Her father had moved to a home near the university for convenience when they'd left Appleton for Fort

Worth. She didn't remember much about the house of those early years with her mother.

Rachel came to live with them after her mother died. The older woman was a widow whose only child had died of meningitis. When her father attended medical school, his hours were long and hard. Rachel was the constant adult in the household. She was retired now and living in Galveston. She loved the sea. She'd tried to answer Maddie's questions when she'd first called and told her about her twin. Rachel knew very little, only that she'd needed the job at the perfect time and she loved her kids, as she called Maddie and her brothers, Carter and Grayson.

Maddie pulled out her cell phone and tried her father's number again. It went straight to voice mail—and the mailbox was full. It drove her crazy. Where was he? Surely if he'd been injured the authorities would have notified her.

If her brothers weren't out of touch as well, she'd see what strings Grayson could pull to locate their dad. But he was working under-cover in some narcotics investigation for Fort

Worth Police and Carter was deployed. She was about to burst with the newfound knowledge about her fractured family and had no one to share it with. Or to find out more about what had caused the siblings to split.

She led Darcy to the room the family used as an office and suggested they search online for ideas of fun art projects they could do together. Although her mind was still reeling with concern about her family, she set her worries aside and focused instead on giving Darcy her undivided attention.

It was the least that Ty's daughter deserved after all she'd been through.

Ty walked straight into the kitchen late that afternoon. He stopped when he saw the table set, Maddie by the counter, rolling pin in hand. Darcy at her side. The aroma of dinner had his mouth watering instantly. He was hot, sweaty and tired.

"Dinner will be ready in about twenty minutes," Maddie said, "I need to finish these biscuits and pop them into the oven. Does that give you enough time to clean up?"

"Sure." Clean up? He normally washed his hands and ate. Obviously that wasn't going to work now. Was he supposed to dress for dinner? He walked through the kitchen and into his bedroom and bath. A hot shower sounded as good as the hot meal. He'd take one fast, to get back to the kitchen as soon as he could. He'd found the Colby cattle on the neighbor's land and driven them back through the broken fence, then repaired it. After taking a quick tally to make sure he'd recovered all, he'd ridden the perimeter for most of the afternoon. The day had been hot, and he knew he smelled of horse, cattle, dirt and sweat.

When they sat down to dinner a short time later, Ty studied his nanny. She'd lasted the day and didn't seem to have a hair out of place. Her clothes weren't suitable to ranching, but they still looked as fresh as they had that morning. How did she do it?

Once seated, Maddie held out her hand to him and reached across the table to take Darcy's. He looked at them.

"Will you bless the food?" Maddie asked.

His mind went blank for a moment. Then

he glanced at Darcy who was watching him. Nodding, he took her hand and Darcy's and bowed his head. He was not given to praying aloud, yet how would they know when he was finished if he didn't? Clearing his throat, he began, "Lord, thank You for the food that's been prepared for us, for providing it and sending Maddie to cook it. Thank You for bringing Darcy home. Amen."

"This isn't my home," Darcy said.

"Darcy, we discussed this," Maddie explained gently, serving the child's plate. "You live here with your dad now."

Ty swallowed a knot in his throat. "What did you two do today?" he asked gruffly.

"We did art projects and made cookies at Violet's house," Darcy piped up. "Chocolate chip. I got to help."

Ty nodded, relieved to see his little girl smiling again. It broke his heart that she felt so displaced. He waited until they'd both filled their plates, then heaped the stew onto his own.

"What did you do?" Maddie asked after a

moment of silence. This man could take the strong silent type to the highest degree.

"Checked on some fencing, got caught up on other things around."

"I need to talk to you later," Maddie said.

His eyes narrowed. "About?"

"The job," she said pointedly.

"Didn't we already talk about that?" he asked.

"If you count keeping her safe and occupying her time, yes, we did. I had in mind a bit more." She hoped he'd agree to discuss it further. The more she was around Ty, the more she liked him. He was honest and straightforward. No artifice around him. It had an appeal that surprised her. She wanted to learn as much about him as she could.

"After Darcy's in bed?" he suggested.

"Fine with me." She had a mental list, maybe she should jot everything down so she didn't forget something. She wasn't sure she wanted two meetings back-to-back with him. One would be challenging enough.

Once dinner was finished, Maddie and Darcy made short work of cleaning the kitchen. Then Ty suggested they walk to the barn with him. Darcy looked at Maddie first, then nodded.

When they reached the corrals where some of the horses were, Darcy climbed the rail fence and, hugging the top rail, gazed at the horses.

"She needs to learn to ride," Maddie said when Ty stood behind Darcy, watching her watch the horses.

"If you ride, too," Darcy said quickly.

"I don't know about that." Though Violet urged her to ride every day, she wasn't comfortable on the back of a horse—unlike her sister, who seemed to move as one with the large animals. The few times she'd gone riding, she'd clutched the saddle horn for dear life.

"If he would teach me, I want to ride that one," Darcy said, pointing to a smaller horse dozing near the far fence. "It's not so big."

"Rambo," Ty said in his deep voice.

"Rambo? Not a child's horse, then," she said, looking at the animal. Not so big? It looked huge to her.

"Misnomer. He's a gentle ride. He'd be good to learn on—for both of you."

She inhaled sharply. "Me?"

"You want to learn and not be so afraid, don't you?"

So he'd seen her riding. She felt her face flush with embarrassment. "Yes, I'd like to learn." She'd never be as at home on a horse as her sister, but if she was going to be here for a few more weeks, she might as well get some practice in.

To Maddie's surprise, they spent a pleasant time walking around in the cooling evening. Ty didn't talk much, but answered every question Darcy asked. Maddie was pleased the child didn't seem at all intimidated by her father. She still looked at him like she was trying to make up her mind about him. But by the end of their walk, she held his hand heading back to the house.

When Maddie suggested a bath before bed, Darcy jumped at the chance.

"We'll call you when she's ready for bed," Maddie said as they went to the part of the house that held two bedrooms and a bath.

In bed before eight-thirty, Darcy looked up at her with her big brown eyes, so like her father's. Did Ty see that resemblance?

Maddie asked if she wanted to hear a story. "Since you don't have any books, I'll make one up if you like."

"Oh, yes," Darcy said with a surprised smile.

Maddie sat on the mattress and began one of the stories she remembered from when she'd been a child. Rachel had often read to her, but she also made up the most fascinating stories of a magical princess. Trying to remember all the ins and outs of the long-running story from her childhood, Maddie began. When Darcy's eyes drooped, she kissed her cheek. "I'll tell you more tomorrow night," she whispered.

She went to find Ty before Darcy fell asleep so he could kiss her good-night and tuck her in.

He wasn't in the house. Hesitant to leave Darcy unattended, Maddie went out the back door and walked around to the front. He sat on a chair on the small porch, working saddle soap into reins.

"She asleep?" he asked.

"No, waiting for you to tuck her in."

He stared at her for a long moment, then looked away.

"It's easy. Go in and kiss her good-night and smooth the covers around her," she said a moment later when he made no move to rise.

He nodded once and stood. After placing the leather on the deck, he stepped past her to the door. "I'm not good at this," he said, so softly she didn't know if she was supposed to hear or not.

She listened to his footsteps as he went back to Darcy's room. "Lord, seems we both need your help here. Please, let Ty grow more comfortable around his daughter. And help me every day I watch her that I say and do the right things."

Maddie sat on the bench by the front wall.

Ty stepped out onto the small porch a moment later. Seeing her, he went to stand next to the bench, resting one boot on the edge, leaning an arm against his raised leg.

"So what did you want to talk about?" he asked.

"I need more specifics about my position."

"Didn't we already cover this at breakfast?" he asked impatiently. "You're to watch Darcy. For however long you stay."

"What does that mean?"

"You're smart, you figure it out."

She watched him in silence for a few minutes, wishing she knew what he was talking about. The man intrigued her, but puzzled her even more. She shook her head. "Sorry, you're going to have to spell it out."

"You've already lasted at the ranch longer than I thought you would."

"Meaning?"

"There's not a lot of excitement for a city girl. You'll be heading back to the bright lights before long once the novelty wears off. I want to know if you can hang on long enough for Darcy to start school."

"I'm having a great time visiting here. Granted, my apartment and all is in Fort Worth, but my family's here."

"New family. Amazing, the resemblance between you and Violet."

She arched a brow. "We're twins."

He nodded. "When Violet suggested you help Darcy I thought she was crazy, but it made sort of sense. Darcy's been raised in a city. I know ranching life is different." He exhaled slowly. "Maybe you can help her transition."

"What do you have in mind?"

He looked over at her again. "For one thing, try to get her to see the advantages of living here. She seems to like the animals. If she learns to ride, I'll get her a pony of her own. Maybe a dog. I bet Violet would let her gather eggs and feed the pigs. Get her used to being here. You can relate—you're city through and through."

"Which doesn't mean I don't realize the advantages of living here."

"You both need more suitable clothes," he said. "She needs jeans and boots to learn to ride. Long-sleeved shirts to protect her arms. A hat for shade."

Maddie noticed his glance at her own

clothes. They were not suitable for the rough-and-tumble of ranching. Not that she was riding or punching cattle. Momentarily sidetracked, she wondered what punching cattle even meant.

"Ranch kids start helping as soon as they can walk, with chores suitable for their ages." He gazed at her. "She can do dishes, right? I'd like you to encourage her to make her bed, make sure her clothes are taken care of."

Maddie nodded. "We'll need to go shopping. You do know she doesn't have anything from home except what social services packed that day. What happened to the furnishings and toys and clothes and all from the apartment?"

"I don't know and don't care," he said curtly.

"A little girl has cherished toys, favorite books, special clothes. It would help her adjust to have familiar things around."

He thought about it for a minute. "I'll contact social services and see what they tell me. I never thought about it, to tell the truth. One minute I'm doing my job, the next minute I find out I'm a father. And have been for eight years, which my ex-wife conveniently forgot to tell me. Thinking about Darcy's stuff was the last thing on my mind."

"I know." Maddie was silent for a moment. Then she looked at him.

"We have a lot in common, don't we?"

"Like?" He frowned. She could tell he didn't like the idea.

"You never knew about Darcy, and I never knew about Violet or Jack or Belle."

"True. But that's all," he said quickly.

Maddie knew he didn't like her—was it because she reminded him of his ex-wife?

Was he against all people who lived in cities? That would be dumb.

"I like it here," she said simply.

His jaw clenched. "For now," he countered.

She stood up and faced him. He put his foot on the ground and crossed his arms in front of his chest. He stood several inches taller than she did and when he narrowed his eyes, as he was doing now, he could be very intimidating. However, she'd caught a hint of vulnerability a couple of times, which gave her courage to say,

"I'm not Darcy's mother. You can't judge me by what happened between you two. Maybe I was raised in the city, but I like it here fine. If I thought I could fit in, I might consider staying."

"No one's asked you to," he said.

Maddie nodded. There was that. And her recent work history was on a magazine, hardly conducive to working on a ranch.

"Still, don't judge me by her."

"Early days yet."

"You are the most stubborn man, you know that?"

A glimmer of amusement showed in his eyes. "So I've been told," he replied.

Maddie was captivated by that glimmer. So he did have a sense of humor. She never would have thought insulting him would almost result in a smile.

He cleared his throat. "Darcy's mother hated the routine of ranching, the constant need to care for the animals. Even the weather. Mostly she hated the idea of being isolated," he explained.

Maddie was longing to ask questions about

his marriage, but refrained. It was not any business of hers. She knew enough—they'd had a child Ty had not known about. And now his ex-wife was dead. Too young to die.

But then her own mother had been too young to die. And she'd been too young to lose her mother.

She couldn't bear to think Darcy might become alone in the world if something happened to her father. Of course she'd heard mention of grandparents. Surely they'd step in if needed.

"Take Darcy into town tomorrow and buy her some suitable clothes," Ty said.

Maddie looked at him again. "You'll need to come as well."

"I don't do shopping."

She smiled. "Obviously you do or there'd be no food in the house or clothes on your back. We won't be long, but you'll know what she needs better than I will. And you can tell me what to get for me as well. We'll have a shopping spree," she said with a wide smile. She loved shopping.

He stared at her as if she'd lost her marbles.

Maddie giggled. "It'll be fun. Think of it as a bonding experience with your daughter."

"Put it that way, I'll go. But we only need to stop at the Feed and Grain. They have all we'll need."

"Works for me." Her heart beat faster thinking about spending time with Ty tomorrow. And Darcy, of course. He'd surprised her by agreeing to go. Still, she knew he was making a serious effort to get to know his daughter and applauded him for it.

"I'm going now. What time should I be here in the morning?" she asked.

"I'd like an early start on chores—especially if I'm leaving for part of the day. Six?"

She nodded, wishing she could sleep in a little later. But she was out to prove to this man that she could do the job. "Six'll be fine. See you then."

She walked slowly back to the main house, thinking about Ty. He was definitely a competent ranch foreman, but she could see he was lost when dealing with Darcy. She hoped she could help them both.

Violet sat in the living room, leafing through a magazine when Maddie entered.

"So how was the first day on the job? I missed you at dinner," Violet said, patting the sofa next to her in silent invitation.

"Things went okay. I'll probably be eating most of my meals there with Darcy. Which is fine with me. It gives me a chance to cook." Maddie crossed to the sofa and sat beside her twin. "Where's Landon?"

"On some phone call he couldn't miss."

Since Landon and Violet had become engaged, he split his time between the ranch and Fort Worth, where he worked. He was currently overseeing plans to remodel the guesthouse on the ranch and talked about moving his company here permanently after they were married. At one time, it was odd for Maddie to imagine Landon living away from the hustle and bustle of Fort Worth. But he'd changed since falling in love with her sister. She prayed everything would work out for the best for them both.

"What can you tell me about Ty that would help me?" she asked.

When Violet had introduced her to all the ranch hands her first few days visiting, she'd said he'd worked for them for eight years. She had to know more than Maddie did.

"He's a good worker. Has a quick mind and is practical. Gets on with the men."

"That doesn't tell me a lot. I could have guessed that by his position. I mean, tell me more about him as Darcy's dad so I know how to help with his daughter."

Violet thought a moment. "I don't know a lot about him, outside of how he works around the ranch. He used to ride rodeos, but got hurt and stopped. He keeps to himself a lot. He became a Christian shortly after starting work here. I don't ever remember hearing he was dating anyone." She shrugged. "I think you should check with Jack—he knows him better. A guy thing, I guess."

Maddie wasn't as comfortable around Jack as she was around Violet. Still, this was for Darcy's benefit. Maybe she could catch him in a talkative mood one of these days. If he hung around the ranch for longer than a day at a time.

Jack had been gone frequently since she'd arrived. He used the fact that he was doing construction work on one of the parcels of the ranch a distance away from here as an excuse for being MIA.

But she knew there was more to it than that. Clearly, the change wasn't any easier on him than on her.

"Ty and I'll be taking Darcy into town tomorrow to buy clothes more suitable for a ranch. I thought I'd pick up some for myself while I'm there," Maddie said.

"You know you're welcome to borrow anything of mine you like," Violet said.

Maddie had already borrowed jeans and old boots the few times she'd ventured out on a horse. She liked her clothes better, but they were very impractical on the dusty ranch.

"I know, thanks. But it's time to get some of my own."

"Stop in at the Simmons Coffee Shop for lunch. Darcy'll like that. Then try the feed store. It carries a lot of Western clothes and boots and hats. All sizes and the prices are reasonable. Otherwise, if you shop at Campbells, the other clothing store in town, you'll find the prices higher than really warranted."

"Want to go in with us?" It would make things easier with Ty if she had a buffer.

"I would, but I was there today. I'm visiting Mom tomorrow. Speaking of which, did you reach your dad yet?"

"Nope, mailbox full, still not answering." Maddie looked at her. "And isn't he *our* dad?"

Shortly before noon the next day, Ty, Maddie and Darcy entered the Simmons Coffee Shop on Main Street. Maddie was still mildly surprised to find it was larger inside than it looked from the street. Tables, booths and the counter all offered seating for customers. Ty chose a booth next to the window so Darcy could also look outside. He had her sit by the window and he slid onto the bench seat next to her. Maddie sat opposite.

Gwen Simmons came over and handed them each a menu. "How are y'all doing today, Ty, Maddie? Can I get you something to drink?" the owner asked as she smiled at them.

"Doing fine, you?" Ty replied.

"Can't complain, wouldn't do any good if I did." She smiled at Darcy. "And who is this fine young lady?"

"My daughter, Darcy," Ty said, opening the menu and avoiding Gwen's surprised look.

"Well, welcome to Grasslands, Darcy. You on a visit?"

Darcy shook her head. "My mommy died, and now I live with him," she said.

Gwen glanced at Maddie, a questioning look in her expression.

"I'm acting as nanny for the time being."

"I know Violet's glad you're staying longer," Gwen said. The older woman seemed to know everyone in the place, and sounded as if she knew what was going on around town as well.

Ty ordered iced tea. Maddie had the same and Darcy ordered chocolate milk. Once their lunch order was taken, Ty sat back and looked out the window.

Maddie wished he'd initiate some kind of conversation. The silence stretched out as she gazed around the room, out the window.

Okay, if he wouldn't, then she would. "Do you come here often?"

He looked at her, his dark eyes a rich, deep brown. She could look at him all day.

"No. Usually working. Unless there's a special reason to come into town at night, it's easier to eat at home."

"I like it," Darcy said. She smiled at Maddie and then looked at her father with hesitation. "It's not so fancy like the restaurants Mom took me to. I had to be real careful and mind my manners."

"You have to mind your manners anywhere," Ty reminded her.

"Mmm," she said, turning to look out the window again.

When the bell over the door jangled, announcing another customer, Maddie looked around and saw Sadie Johnson. She waved at the new church secretary whom she'd met at church two weeks ago. Sadie nodded, hesitated a moment and then walked over.

Maddie watched her and wondered why she always wore baggy clothing. She wasn't overweight. And the big glasses could be swapped for a more stylish pair—or even contacts. Would Sadie be open to some well-meant suggestions?

"Hi," Sadie said with a shy smile.

Ty slid out of the booth and stood. "Sadie," he said.

"Here for lunch, I see. Who's this?" she asked, looking at Darcy.

"My daughter, Darcy," Ty responded. "Darcy, this is Sadie Johnson—she's the church secretary."

"You're new to town, too," Maddie said with a friendly smile. "So am I and so is Darcy."

"We're going shopping after lunch," Darcy said.

"That'll be nice. Enjoy your lunch," Sadie said with a timid smile. She turned and headed for the counter.

Ty slid back onto the seat. "Guess Darcy and I need to start going to church come Sunday."

"Don't you normally?" Maddie asked.

He shrugged. "I try to make it most of the time. Sometimes there're things at the ranch that need attention that can't wait. Jeb's a good preacher. First I've known."

This was more information than he'd revealed in all the short time she'd known him.

"Why's that?"

"Didn't know the Lord until a few years ago," he said gruffly.

Maddie wondered why that was. She couldn't remember when she didn't have a close relationship with Jesus. Rachel had not only been there to take care of them when their father was studying and working, she'd brought all of them to the Lord. What a blessing she'd been to Maddie's life.

"Can I get jeans and boots and a cowboy hat?" Darcy asked. "Then I'll be ready to ride a horse."

Ty looked at her and nodded, his expression softening slightly. Maddie loved watching Ty interact with his daughter. Sometimes he looked baffled, other times charmed. She liked it most when he smiled—at Darcy or her. Especially when he smiled at her.

Maddie wished she knew what to do to

bring the two of them closer. Time would help. But it was hard to sit by and do nothing.

Darcy looked at her. "If you buy boots and a hat, you can ride, too. He can teach you."

Ty looked at Maddie, a hint of amusement in his eyes.

"That's all it takes," he said.

Maddie laughed. "If only. I'll see what's there. No guarantee that because I dress the part, I'll be a cowgirl," she said to Darcy.

Ty shook his head, the amusement vanishing. "No. Highly unlikely, I'd say."

Annoyed she'd said anything, Maddie didn't know how to convince him he could trust her not to run back to Fort Worth anytime soon.

Time would help with that as well.

"Can we buy a storybook?" Darcy asked. "Maddie's telling me the bestest story, but I want her to read me some books Mommy used to like," Darcy said.

"That can be arranged," Ty said.

Their food arrived and the next few minutes were devoted to eating.

It was awkward being the only one making conversation, so Maddie was glad for the diversion of their lunch. Once finished, they'd be heading to the store.

The Feed and Grain was on the edge of town. Ty turned into the huge gravel parking lot and pulled up to the wide wooden porch, which ran the full width of the building and contained stacked dog crates, rolls of wire fencing of various heights, a small enclosed area with baby chicks and an assortment of decorative items for a garden.

To the side was a cavernous, barnlike warehouse loaded with hay, straw, alfalfa and brown sacks Maddie hadn't a clue what they were. A forklift was maneuvering bales of hay into the back of a pickup.

Inside, the building was clearly divided into clothing and items for livestock, fencing and chicken feed. They headed to the clothing side. Shelves reaching the ceiling held boxes of boots of all varieties and sizes, work shoes and cowboy hats. Racks of clothing included jeans, long, dark duster raincoats, colorful shirts in all sizes and denim jackets.

"Wow," Maddie said. "One-stop shopping for Western wear."

Ty looked at her, then around the store. "I've been shopping here the last eight years. Nothing fancy, but good, practical clothing. What size does she wear?" he asked, heading to the edge where children's clothing was displayed.

Maddie picked up his vibe—the sooner they got this over with, the sooner they could return home. "I don't know. She'll probably have to try a few things on so we can gauge that. Once we know her size, we can go from there."

The three of them looked at the different shirts. Maddie held several Darcy liked up to her, judging her size. Satisfied, she draped them over her arm. She thought these would fit the child. They moved on to jeans.

Maddie could feel Ty's impatience grow. He said nothing, but she could tell he didn't like hanging around and discussing which jeans would fit and be suitable for the ranch. Maddie understood to a point. Jeans were jeans, but some were fancier than others. She hesitated over a pair that had rhinestones on the pocket. Somehow she couldn't see Ty Garland being impressed. Not that she necessarily wanted to impress him. Well, maybe a little. Enough so he wouldn't cast her in the same light as his ex-wife.

Fortunately, Darcy liked the plain ones and soon she was trying clothes on in one of the dressing booths at the back of the store. Maddie, knowing her own size, grabbed a few items to try on as well.

Ty leaned against one of the posts holding up the ceiling as he waited for the two to decide if they'd be buying the clothes they selected or not. He didn't know about buying things for a little girl. Grateful for Maddie's assistance, he couldn't help wishing it took less time. When he needed new clothes, he came in, picked up an assortment and left. No trying-on needed.

They still had boots and hats and maybe a jacket or two to get.

When Darcy stepped out of the fitting room a minute later, he felt his heart catch. She looked adorable. The yellow top was perfect with her brown hair. The jeans made her look taller than he'd expected. It wouldn't be too long before she grew up completely. For a moment he was shaken that he'd almost missed all this. Anger against Brittany burned.

"Where's Maddie?" she asked, looking around.

"Right here," she said, stepping out.

He looked at her. For a moment she looked exactly like Violet—jeans, yellow shirt. She'd even pulled her hair behind her ears, which helped with the effect. She may look like Violet sometimes, but he could tell the difference in a heartbeat. Maddie was special, had a manner about her that he found intriguing and appealing. Like now—dressing the part for Darcy. Her sweetness was a balm to him after the hard ending to his marriage. If he didn't know better, he'd think she was a cowgirl from way back, dressed up for some rodeo event.

He looked away. It was highly unlikely she'd ever remain on the ranch. She was a city girl looking for work. No use getting used to her being around. Though he couldn't help stealing a quick glance as she had Darcy turn around, testing the fit at the shoulders and waist. "Perfect. Now that we know your size, we can buy more things without trying them on."

Darcy looked at her. "You look like Violet now," she said, unconsciously echoing Ty's thoughts.

"I always look like her—we're twins," she said.

Darcy shook her head. "Not with the other clothes. Now you look like you belong."

Maddie gave the child a hug. "Thanks. So do you."

"Looks can be deceiving," Ty muttered.

Maddie frowned. "Or not. I may not be a cowgirl from way back, but I can learn."

He shook his head. The jury was still out on that one.

Once they each had a stack of clothes, they moved to try on hats. Fortunately there were a couple of small ones for Darcy, as the first one she tried on fell below her ears and completely covered her eyes.

Boots proved the most difficult to buy. Explaining what to look for and how they should feel was a new experience for Ty. But he didn't want either of them to have problems with the boots, so he took extra time and care to make sure they both got the best.

It was late afternoon by the time they reached the ranch. Ty wanted to check on the men and see if there was anything crucial he needed to deal with, so he left the women at his place and headed out to the barn.

He'd never gone shopping with girls before. He'd loved the expression on Darcy's face when she saw herself completely clothed in jeans, shirt, boots and hat. She'd beamed her delight. He'd felt another clutch in his heart. He'd wanted to sweep her up into his arms, hug her, and promise to never let anything harm her.

That would have freaked her out, he expected. She was still wary around him, as if she couldn't believe he was truly her father. Who blamed her, after Brittany telling her for eight years that he was dead? She hadn't even told Darcy his name. That hurt.

Nothing he could do about the past. He had to move forward and hope before long she'd know they could make a happy family together.

He had to hand it to Maddie. She smoothed everything. Acting as a kind of buffer between him and Darcy, she kept things on an even keel. For a moment he wished she wouldn't return to Fort Worth. That she'd find her place here on the ranch. Frowning at the thought, he tried to banish it. He had work to do, not time to fantasize about a future that was never likely to materialize.

Chapter Three

Maddie and Darcy wore their new Western attire home, both pleased with their selections. They had unloaded the car and were already putting things away when Violet knocked on the door.

"I saw you were home and wanted to see how it went," she said. Then she laughed. "My favorite color is yellow," she informed them, pointing to her pale yellow shirt. Maddie's was the color of buttercups, Darcy's a brighter yellow.

"We look like an ad for butter," Violet said, giving Maddie a hug. "Your shopping spree gives me hope that you'll stay longer."

"I said I'll be staying at least until Darcy starts school," Maddie reminded her.

"I know. And I'm hoping I can convince you to stay even longer."

"We've been through this. I need to work, and there aren't a lot of publishing opportunities in Grasslands."

"There could be other jobs. Never mind that now. I'm happy you bought the jeans and boots." A mischievous glint filled her eyes. "Now we just need to get you comfortable riding," Violet said.

"We *went* riding," Maddie protested. Granted, she couldn't sit a horse like her twin, but then, she hadn't been raised around horses since she was little.

"I'm leaving the next stage to Ty. If he's teaching Darcy, he can teach you," Violet murmured.

Maddie felt her adrenaline spike. If he had his way, he'd not only teach them to ride, he'd have them out on the back forty in no time, herding cattle, avoiding stampedes and fending off rustlers.

She sighed. In for a penny, she thought.

As it drew nearer to dinnertime, Maddie's nerves grew more and more jangled. She'd already spent hours with Ty today. Yet she couldn't help anticipating seeing him again. She'd felt a special connection today as they shopped for Darcy together. She was growing increasingly interested in the cowboy. She hoped he was changing his mind about her. She wasn't just a city sophisticate. She fit on the ranch more and more each day.

Two pairs of boots clomped around the kitchen as she and Darcy prepared dinner—tonight, a roast with all the trimmings. One thing she'd discovered was the huge freezer beside the back stoop filled with various cuts of meat. They'd not go hungry in this house.

Darcy still wore her cowboy hat. She swaggered around, setting the table, and came over to Maddie several times to watch her.

"Today was fun," she said. "Do you think he'll let us go riding after dinner?"

"We'll have to ask," Maddie said. She wasn't so sure she wanted riding lessons. What if she made a fool of herself in front of Ty?

She heard his footsteps on the back porch and it was all she could do to continue slicing the fresh tomato she planned to have with their salads and not turn around to watch him enter. Every cell attuned to him, she tried to be as casual as she could be. But when she heard Darcy greet him, she spun around and added her greeting as well. She was uncertain where she stood with the man. But he fascinated her.

He took off his hat and ran his fingers through his thick hair. Tossing the hat onto a peg on the wall, he looked at her. His dark eyes seemed to delve right into her.

"Something smells nice," he said. He looked at Maddie from the yellow top down to the brown boots, then looked at Darcy. His face softened in a smile as he looked at the miniature cowgirl. "You both look real nice. Still wearing that hat?"

"I'm a cowgirl. I have to wear a hat," Darcy explained.

"Mostly, it's needed to shade your face from the sun," Ty said gently. "But it's okay to wear inside. It looks like you're ready to ride the range."

He hadn't moved from the door and Maddie wondered if he felt out of place in his own home. It couldn't be easy to go from being a longtime single man to coming home to a house with two females.

"I don't know how to ride," Darcy reminded him.

"We'll get you up to speed in no time. It's easy," he said, glancing at Maddie.

"Don't look at me. I've been on a horse only a few times, that's about as far as I've progressed." She threw up her hands. "You're looking at two hopeless city girls. Despite having the stockyards and all in Fort Worth, no one I know there actually *owns* a horse."

His expression went hard. Maddie knew he remembered his wife. She wished she could retrieve the words she'd thoughtlessly spoken.

"But we're both willing to learn. Violet said you could teach us," she said, hoping mentioning Violet's ringing endorsement of his equestrian skills would encourage Ty to spend more time with Darcy.

"We'll get started after dinner."

Maddie forced a smile. "That'll be great. My sister wants me to become as acclimated to the ranch as you want Darcy to become. You get two students for the price of one."

"Won't that be fun?" He scowled.

Turning so he wouldn't see the amusement on her face, she resumed slicing the tomato. He spoke with Darcy, his voice gentling somewhat as he explained they could pick out some horses after dinner. She herself wouldn't mind waiting a few more days, or weeks. But sooner or later she had to become more comfortable or she'd lose out on an important part of her sister's life.

Ty was expecting to say the blessing tonight. It had never been a part of family life when he was growing up. Of course, nothing much but booze and anger had been part of his childhood life. He tried to forget, but with Darcy around, he couldn't help but contrast the two of them. He vowed he'd do all he could to protect his little girl. And raise her up right. He was not his father and never wanted to be.

Dinner passed pleasantly enough with

Darcy encouraged by Maddie to talk some more, sharing her best part of the day.

Her fit of giggles one time touched Ty's heart. He'd like to hear that all the time. He glanced at Maddie, who was smiling indulgently at the child. She still looked more polished and sophisticated than the women he knew around the various ranches in the area, but at least she was making an effort to fit in. The yellow shirt suited her—looking as pretty as the fancy silk shirts she normally wore. The cotton, however, was much more practical. Maybe it wasn't the clothes so much as how she wore them.

Once dinner was finished and the dishes were done, the three of them headed out to the barn.

The hush of the early evening was everywhere. The men were still in the bunkhouse eating. The horses had been fed and were now dozing in the corral. He heard the bleat of the goat, but didn't see her. Two of the horses ambled over to the rail fence and hung their heads over. When he reached them, Ty idly scratched their heads.

Ty had no idea how to teach two girls of different ages how to ride. He couldn't remember when he hadn't known how to ride. As far as he remembered, his first time he'd got on and held on until he got the hang of it. Yeah, that'd be great with both of them. He didn't want either to get hurt.

To the side of the barn, one of the other cowboys was hosing down Stoney, the gelding he'd ridden that day.

"He likes that," Ty said, watching the horse move to get more water from the hose.

"It's like he's in a shower," Darcy said, laughing.

"So, which is the gentlest, sweetest horse you have?" Maddie asked, looking through the rails at the horses in the corral. One more ambled over and put his head over the top rail.

Ty scratched around his ears while he decided which horse would be the best for Maddie. He wasn't too worried about Darcy. Rambo had two speeds—slow and stop. Maddie had been riding a couple of times, so knew enough to stay on. But he didn't want to risk her falling off.

"Rambo's the best for Darcy."

"Rambo?" Maddie said with some trepidation, even though Ty had assured her that Rambo was gentle.

"Hey, no one knows what a horse is going to be like when it's a foal. His first owners obviously thought he'd be a take-charge champion. He's slow, hard to get into second gear and perfect for a little girl to start on."

"What about a bigger girl?" Maddie asked, tentatively patting the head of one of the horses by the rail.

"Who did you ride before?"

"I think Violet said his name was Shadow—the horse was dark gray."

"And you stayed on, right?"

"Well, he didn't buck. I sat there and held on for dear life."

Ty gave a slow smile. Maddie was gutsy on the outside, but he suspected she was as nervous around horses as Darcy. He looked at her and was surprised at the look on her face.

"You should smile more often," she said softly.

Which instantly wiped the smile from his

face. He went to the barn to get halters and lead ropes.

"Tonight we'll get acquainted. I'll bring them into the barn and you two can groom them, learn how to walk around them, clean their hooves, that kind of thing."

"They're awfully big," Darcy said, moving closer to Maddie.

When Maddie put her arm casually around Darcy's shoulders, Ty felt a pang of longing. He wished his daughter would step closer to him when she was scared. Wished he felt comfortable enough around her to put his arm across her shoulder. Wished he knew if she even wanted him to.

Darcy had worn her hat. Now she had to tip her head back to see him from beneath the brim. "Do they kick or bite?"

"Some do, not the ones we'll be dealing with. Mostly, Jack and I don't put up with horses who don't have good manners. Too distracting." He nodded briskly. "Come on, let's get Rambo first."

The next hour Ty spent going over things with Darcy, and all the while Maddie was hovering over his shoulder. He cross-tied the horse in the center of the barn and brought out the equipment to properly groom him. Darcy started out checking with Maddie for every task he explained to her. As if to verify with the other city girl that it was something she could do.

He tried not to become frustrated. She'd recently lost her mother. She hadn't known about him. She wasn't used to horses or him. But it was getting to him.

Finally, he turned to Maddie. "Maybe this would go better if you weren't here."

"No, Maddie, don't leave," Darcy protested, moving to stand beside her.

"I'm not leaving. And it's going great. Let me have a brush and we'll brush down this side and then you and your dad can brush down the other side while I comb his mane and tail."

Okay, so suggesting Darcy's touchstone leave hadn't been so smart. But Maddie's solution had been. It would unite the two of them in one project. Baby steps, Ty reminded himself.

It was easier dealing with cowboys.

* * *

Once Maddie had Darcy in bed, she walked out onto the front porch where Ty sat contemplating how he didn't feel one bit closer to his daughter despite spending the major portion of the day with her.

"She's excited about grooming the horse and talked about Rambo the entire time she was getting ready for bed," Maddie said as she walked out of the house.

"Didn't seem like it to me," he grumbled. He gestured to the bench, hoping she'd stay a little longer. Give him some pointers, maybe.

She sat on the bench and smiled at him. "I've noticed she's a bit shy around you. The only way past that is for her to get to know you better. Find some common ground." She paused. "So you need to plan activities that you two can do together—to build that parent-child bond."

"Like what?" Ty asked impatiently.

"Like going inside to tuck her in. She's still awake."

Nodding tersely, he rose and went into the house. He wanted to be the one to tuck her in every night, until she got too old for that. But when he stepped into her room, she had her back to the door.

"Darcy?"

"Huh?" She rolled over and looked at him.

"Good night," he said, going down on his knees by her bed and brushing her hair off her forehead. Her cowboy hat was at the foot of her bed, the boots right beside it.

"Thank you for buying me cowboy clothes," she said softly.

"Hey, you have to fit in, right?"

She nodded, her eyes shining. "And when I can ride, I can go all over the ranch with you."

"Yes, you can." He kissed her cheek and smiled. "Sleep well."

"Okay." She rolled over again and he rose to leave. Just before he turned out the light, he looked at his daughter. He was still amazed he'd fathered a child, and she had captured his heart the first time he saw her. He only wanted the best life had to offer for her. She'd had a bad break with her mother dying. *Please, Father, keep this child in the hollow of Your hand,* he silently prayed.

When he stepped out onto the porch, he looked out over the ranch. This was his life, the only one he knew or wanted. "How do I ease a child into this life when she's used to apartment living and being supervised all the time? I have to work. I can't take off to be with her all the time until she's grown," he said as he rejoined Maddie on the bench.

"She'll come around. Don't forget, it's less than two weeks ago that everything in her life changed. Children are resilient. She'll gradually get used to things, and in a few months will hardly remember her first days here."

Maddie looked at her boots, then looked up at him and grinned. "I feel like a cowgirl today."

"You might look the part, but once the novelty wears off, you'll leave," he said, but he took a look at her happy expression and wished he'd kept quiet. If she wanted to play dress-up for a while, he didn't care. It wasn't as if he was planning on her staying. Once burned, twice shy.

"Umm, maybe you're right or maybe you're

wrong. Only time will tell, won't it?" she asked easily.

They sat in companionable silence for a few minutes, then Ty's curiosity got the better of him.

"So how does it feel to suddenly discover the other half of your family?" he asked. Maybe Darcy felt the same and it would help if he knew how to respond.

"Weird, mostly. And frustrating. I have a thousand questions and no answers. Belle is my mother, if she's Violet's, there's no question about that. Yet all my life I thought Sharla was. It's her name on my birth certificate."

"Maybe she adopted you. Doesn't the state change birth records in cases of adoption?" he asked.

"I guess. But why didn't I ever know that? I thought the current thinking was adopted children should know that all along."

"Did you ask your father?"

"I've been trying to reach him for five weeks. Dad takes off on missionary trips for weeks at a time. He's a doctor and provides medical care in poverty-stricken areas here and abroad. Last I heard he was heading down near the border. He's never been one to check in often, but this is the longest I can remember him being incommunicado." She sighed. "Even if I reached him, there's no telling what he'll say."

"No one else knows?"

"I asked our longtime housekeeper, the woman who came when our mother died. Rachel was astonished to learn about Violet. She didn't have a clue. She only knew our mother had died before she came to stay with us. I tried calling my brother Grayson, but he's a cop and working undercover somewhere so hasn't called me back yet. And my other brother is deployed. I didn't want to worry him about all this. Besides, he'll know less than I do. I just wish my dad would return my call."

"Or that Belle would recover consciousness," he said. He knew his entire family history. No gaps, no mysterious partings. He wondered what it must be like for Maddie to have so many unanswered questions.

"Does Darcy have grandparents on your side?" Maddie asked suddenly.

He shook his head. "They're all dead and gone."

"Oh, I'm sorry."

He shrugged. "No need. My old man was a mean drunk. My mother left me and my brother with him when I was a kid. Never heard from her again. When he tied one on once he about killed my brother. He ended up in prison and then dead from some prison yard fight."

"And your brother?"

"Died a few years ago from a drug deal gone bad. He was a cop like your brother, worked in Houston."

"Oh." She was silent. Ty wondered what she was thinking.

"I don't drink," he added.

Her eyes looked soft in the fading light as she looked at him. "I don't, either. But not because of my dad. I'm sorry you didn't have the best of childhoods."

"I got by."

"Grayson and Carter and I were lucky. We had Rachel."

"Grayson's Jack's twin, right?"

She nodded. "And won't he be surprised when he finds out he has a twin. I wish we could have answers by then. On the other hand, maybe he can dig something up."

"Big-brother worship," Ty said, teasing. He watched to make sure she took it right.

Maddie laughed. "I suppose. He is my hero. He was my mainstay when Mom died. I was about five, younger even than Darcy. I was so lost. Hard to believe now, because I love Rachel, but I was not going to accept her when she came to stay with us. I wanted my mother."

"So do you think that's what Darcy's feeling? She won't accept anyone including me because she wants her mother?" he asked.

"I don't know enough about children to voice an opinion," she admitted. "I know with patience and love, Rachel conquered each of us. We had a happy childhood once we got over our mother's death. There were a few rocky times, but overall it was due to Rachel that we all turned out as well as we have."

"And your father," he said.

She sat in silence for a while. "Not so much. He had to study constantly to become a doctor. You know what arduous hours interns and residents keep. If it hadn't been for Rachel I don't know what we would have done. This situation is so frustrating. I so want to talk to someone who knows something."

"You have Violet."

"She's as ignorant of the past as I am. Which reminds me, I think you should do something about getting Darcy's stuff. Did you call social services about her favorite toys, books, clothes? A picture of her mother?"

Ty felt himself close up. He didn't want a picture of Brittany around.

He felt the soft touch of Maddie's hand on his arm. He looked at her.

"For all her faults, she was Darcy's mother and the little girl loved her. For her sake, see if you can obtain a photograph for her to keep in her room."

"Call social services in the morning and see what we'd need to do," he said.

"Do you think they'll talk to me about it?"

"Tell them you have my permission." He stood up. "It's been a long day. I'm turning in."

She rose as well and looked at him in the faint light spilling from the window. "I'm going to be a bit presumptuous here, but I think you need to forgive her. For withholding Darcy from you."

He looked up at the stars for a moment, then sighed. "I know it's the right thing to do. The Lord has forgiven me for all my faults and sins. But I'm having a hard time with it. I get so frustrated, I want to punch something."

Maddie touched him again. He moved his arm until he could clasp her hand. It felt small and soft in his. Sweetly feminine.

"No one said it would be easy, but it's needed. For you, most of all. I'll pray with you if you like," Maddie offered.

She wore her faith for all to see and share. He was still new enough to know he had miles to go before he could be an outstanding example of Christ. Yet her simple gestures, like this, like the blessing before the meal, made him want to be as open and faithful as she.

"Shoot," he said, closing his eyes, holding her hand.

"Lord, we thank You for today. We appreciate all the blessings You've sent to our lives. Lord, we ask You to bestow forgiveness in our hearts toward Brittany for keeping the knowledge of Darcy from Ty. She's a precious gift and we are so thankful she's come to live here. Help Ty forgive the wrong and find a way to his daughter's heart. In the name of our Savior, we pray."

Maddie gave his hand a squeeze, then withdrew hers and bid him good-night.

Ty watched as she headed for the main house. His gaze was drawn again to the sky overhead. "Lord, what she said. Let me know how to bond with Darcy. I'm not sure I'm the right man for her, but I'll do my best to become the best dad in this world. Show me the way, please, Father."

Ty looked once more toward the main house. Maddie had already gone inside. He hoped she'd stay around until school started. Was he wrong about her? He was beginning to think so. She had been perfect with Darcy. And seemed to like being with him—or was he seeing something that wasn't there? He liked being with her, which surprised him to no end. Who would have thought it? It was early days yet, but Maddie was growing on him. Maybe— Maybe nothing. He turned to enter his home. She was here for Darcy. He'd do well to remember that.

Sunday morning Maddie dressed with care for church. She chose one of her favorite yellow dresses. Soft and flowing, it was cool enough for the heat, yet the cap sleeves gave a hint of protection against the coolness in the church. She wore high-heeled yellow sandals and let her hair fall free. She'd pulled it back into a short ponytail for the past several days to keep it off her neck while she and Darcy learned more and more about riding, and while they helped Violet in the vegetable garden.

She'd made plans last night to attend services with Ty and Darcy, at the child's insistence. Despite spending time together every evening, father and daughter still weren't comfortable around each other without Maddie in the middle. Sometimes she felt like an interpreter. Ty would say something, and Darcy would get mad. But once Maddie explained what he meant, Darcy would be fine. Then Darcy would do something Ty didn't like, and he'd get frustrated. Maddie would clarify and things would be fine.

It got exhausting after a while. Somehow she wanted to bring them closer without constantly intervening, but at least they were gradually getting to know each other.

And she was gaining a new perspective of Ty Garland. She was honored he'd confided some of his family history to her. Her heart ached for anyone who didn't have a happy childhood. Knowing about his dysfunctional past and his broken marriage—not to mention his ex-wife's keeping their daughter from him—would give any man reason to be distrustful. She hoped she could prove to him that he could count on her.

She entered Ty's small house through the front door after a perfunctory knock. Ty had told her to treat the place as her own, but she never forgot to whom it belonged.

Heading for Darcy's room, Maddie was startled to see the child dressed in her jeans and new pink shirt, putting on her boots.

"Good morning," she said, crossing the room and giving the child a hug and kiss on her cheek. "You look like a rose in pink. But I think something else might be more suitable for church. Those are your work clothes."

"These are my new clothes and I like them. I want everybody in church to know I know how to be a cowgirl." She stuck out her lower lip. "Besides, he's wearing jeans, so I can, too."

Oops. Maddie had noticed at church the last few weeks that many of the younger people wore more casual attire. And she'd always been able to spot the cowboys and ranchers by their dress jeans and polished boots. She hadn't really paid that much attention to what people wore. Rachel always had them dress nicely to respect the Lord. It was ingrained into her now, but in truth, the Lord probably didn't care as long as the person showed up.

Ty came to the door. "Is there a problem?"

Maddie looked over at him. He was wearing jeans, but they looked brand-new. The boots he wore weren't the ones he had on last night. These were polished enough to please her marine brother. The white shirt and bolo tie were so typical of Texans.

"Is this okay for Darcy to wear?" she asked.

Ty looked at Darcy. "Why wouldn't it be?" He then studied Maddie for a moment, making her feel like a bug beneath a microscope. "Not everyone dresses to the nines for church. This is a small town. Neighbors aren't out to impress neighbors."

She narrowed her eyes. "Are you saying I am?"

"Hey, city girl, that attire might make it in Dallas, but it's a bit over-the-top here."

"Fort Worth," she said with disdain. "Not Dallas. And it's perfectly acceptable to dress up a little for church. I go to worship and honor God. Why shouldn't I look my best?"

"I'm looking my best." Darcy stomped in her boots and grinned. "I'll wear my hat, too."

"As long as you take it off in church," Ty said.

Maddie started to say something, then stopped. For once it was Darcy and Ty against her. She smiled. "I can tell when you two are ganging up on me." Perfect, their first united front.

Ty grinned at Darcy. "I guess we know more about the lifestyle here than the city girl, right?"

"Right!" She marched proudly over to her father. "I'm ready to go."

The three of them caused a few heads to turn when they entered the local community church a short time later. The last three Sundays, Maddie had entered with Violet and that had caused heads to turn at the novelty of the long-lost twins reunited.

Today, comments flew because she wasn't with Violet. She spotted her twin sitting near the front with Landon.

She was glad when Ty stopped at a row only partway up the aisle. She entered the pew first, moving halfway in to sit beside a family of four with two children about Darcy's age. Darcy came next to her and then Ty. Noticing the clothing of the family to her left, she realized she was a bit overdressed compared to their jeans and cotton shirts.

Fortunately, in looking around, she saw several other ladies who were dressed up. One older woman even wore a fancy hat with netting and white gloves! Rachel would love her. Maybe she should tell Ty to be glad she didn't dress up to that degree.

She saw Sadie sitting in the front pew. Also near the front sat Gwen and Gabe Simmons from the café. Maddie knew she'd have to be here longer to know many people, but at least she recognized a few.

Maddie loved the hymns chosen for the day. She shared her hymnal with Darcy and could clearly hear Ty's strong voice singing the familiar songs. It gave her a thrill to hear his voice so strong in conviction.

The sermon was on the prodigal son. Listening to the pastor's explanation of forgiveness and love, she hoped some of it would resonate with Ty and his situation. She offered up a silent prayer for her employer and his child, trusting the Lord to bring everything about to His glory. She added her own petition to discover the facts of her own past and a request to heal Belle and have her father get in touch. And for her to forgive them both for whatever had split their family.

When church ended, Ty and Darcy moved toward the back with the rest of the congregation while Maddie waited near the aisle to speak to Violet and Landon. When they drew abreast, Violet reached out and hugged her.

"Love your dress."

"Ty thinks I'm showing off—city-girl style," Maddie said, falling into step with them. "He certainly isn't big on anyone who wasn't born and bred to ranch life."

"Once burned, twice shy. As long as you watch his daughter, what do you care what he thinks?" Violet asked.

Maddie didn't want to voice her interest in the ranch foreman. Was it the appeal of someone so totally different from anyone else she knew? No, it was more than being different.

There was some special spark between them. She was happier being with him than being apart. He appealed to her on a basic level. He was a strong man who wasn't afraid to ask for help. His values seemed in line with hers. And he was the cutest thing she'd ever seen. But even Jack was easier to understand than Ty.

"Violet. Maddie." Sadie hovered behind the last row of pews, beckoning them over.

"What's up?" Violet asked. Landon greeted her politely, then told Violet he'd wait outside.

"Your mother's listed as the coordinator of the church picnic. Pastor Jeb asked if I'd check with you to see if you could take over in her absence." She bit her lip nervously. "You know everyone, Violet, and I'm still trying to get names straight. As I understand it, Belle made some plans before the accident, now everyone's sort of floundering and the picnic's in three weeks."

"I don't know," Violet said slowly. "I already have a full plate. Between running the teen youth center, working at the truck farm and helping out at the ranch, I barely have a second to spare. And when I do, I'm off visiting Mom." She sighed. "I'd like to help, but I'm not sure I'd have the time to do a good job."

"What's involved? Maybe I could help," Maddie offered.

Sadie's face brightened. "Oh, that would be great. Actually, everything was divvied up and people have been working on their tasks. We need someone to check with all the committee chairmen to verify things are going along as they are supposed to, and then oversee the actual picnic day. It'll be out at Fraser Lake, where it's been held the last ten years or so, from what I've learned," Sadie explained. "I haven't been here long enough to know what all's involved, and really feel out of my depths. Thank you, Maddie!"

Maddie smiled and nodded. "My pleasure. I worked for three years in the production of the *Texas Today* magazine, and I excel at project management. It will be a challenge, but I'm sure Violet'll help where she can."

"You know it. Nice of you to volunteer," her twin said.

"Here's the folder with the notes I found in

the office. I'm sure there's probably more at the ranch that Belle had," Sadie said. "This is such a relief. I was afraid I would have to step in and this is not something I felt comfortable with. There's so much to learn in my new job, sometimes I feel overwhelmed."

"Maddie, come on. He's waiting," Darcy called from the double doors.

"'He?'" Violet asked, swinging around to look at Darcy.

"She never calls Ty anything but *he*. I've not heard her call him Dad or Ty or anything directly and when talking about him it's always *he*. I hope she warms up to him soon," Maddie said, tucking the file folder beneath her arm.

Maddie gave her sister a quick hug. "I'll check in later to see if there's more information in the ranch office."

"I'll look for it as soon as I get home," Violet said. Turning to Sadie, she smiled. "Don't hesitate to call me if you need any information I might have. I know a new job can be stressful until you get the hang of it. We're just glad Pastor Jeb was able to find someone so quickly after our former secretary had to quit."

Sadie blushed at the mention of the reverend's name, which didn't go unnoticed by the twins.

Maddie bid Violet and Sadie goodbye and hurried to join Darcy, taking her hand in her free one and smiling at the child.

"What's the hurry?" she asked.

"He's waiting. He said he wants to go home."

"Ummm, I have another idea. I'll ask him to take us to where the church picnic is going to be."

"What church picnic?" Darcy looked intrigued.

"Apparently, the church family gets together at a lake for a big picnic each year. I want to know more about it, so maybe your dad can tell us about past years."

Ty was leaning against his truck when they walked over. He didn't look impatient or in a hurry.

"Ready?" he asked.

"Do you know where Fraser Lake is?" Maddie asked.

"Sure, on Tim Fraser's land. Big man-made lake. Why?"

"Is that where the church has its summer picnic?"

He nodded, opening the passenger door and helping Darcy get in. After she scooted over, he turned and held his hand to assist Maddie.

She took it, feeling the hard calluses. It gave her a fluttery feeling, both appealing and disconcerting.

Once she was seated, he closed the door and walked around to get behind the wheel.

"Why the interest?" Ty asked, once in the truck.

"I sort of volunteered to coordinate the picnic. Apparently, Belle was in charge and they put off getting anyone else, hoping she'd recover faster than she has."

He looked at her. "Sounds like it's a lot of work."

"Maybe, but it sounded more like organization was needed. Anyway, I said I'd give it a shot."

"Do you have time for it?" he asked.

"Sure. Darcy can help me," Maddie said with a grin at the young girl.

"I love picnics," the child gushed.

Ty glanced at her, his expression softening slightly. "I didn't know that. We can have a picnic lunch today if you like. Ride out to a shady spot and eat lunch there."

"Can Maddie come?"

"Of course."

"But can we see Fraser Lake first?" Maddie asked.

He shrugged. "It's not on the way, but not too far out of the way, either. It'll mean a later lunch, but sure, we can swing by."

Ty turned left out of town and before long, turned into a long drive that wound through fences lining both sides. Around one bend in the road an old, wooden two-story house came into view. He kept driving beyond it and then came to a stop in a large, packed-dirt field. Directly ahead was the lake. On the banks, here and there were tall shade trees.

"This is larger than I expected," she said, staring at the size of the lake. Probably four or five football fields in size, with grassy sloping land between their parking place and the water and several picnic tables beneath the trees.

"Old man Fraser made it during the forties. He only had the one son—Tim Fraser. He ran cattle for a while, made a killing in the stock market and decided working was more than he wanted to do. So he spends some time here, most of his time in Dallas," Ty explained. "He hired a skeleton crew to keep the few head he still runs. Mostly he lets the town use this lake however it wants. I've only been a member of the church a few years, but know they've had an annual summer picnic here for at least a decade or longer."

"Can we go in the water?" Darcy asked.

"Not today, but when the picnic's going on folks bring little boats, rubber rafts, tire inner tubes and everyone likes to swim. The lake's fed by rain in season and then kept full by a well over on the other side. By late September it's down more than this, but always fills back up during the winter."

"How many people come to this picnic?" Maddie asked, suddenly realizing this task might be larger than she'd expected.

"Most of the families from church and whomever they invite. I'd say we have a couple of hundred people."

"Oh, my." She gazed around. "And there's enough parking?"

Ty nodded.

She counted the picnic tables. "Surely there aren't enough tables for everyone."

"Seems to me folks bring stuff that day like portable tables, blankets, chairs. I came one year with a couple of the ranch hands. We just sat on the ground."

She had a lot to catch up on. Maybe she should have followed Violet's lead and said she didn't have time. But she wanted to help. And what better way to get to know more of the residents of Grasslands?

"Can we go now?" Darcy asked, losing interest once no one made a move to get out of the truck.

"Sure. Let's go get our own picnic today," Ty said.

Maddie was tempted to let Darcy and Ty go on their picnic without her. She wanted to see whatever Violet found about the picnic plans.

When she suggested that to Darcy, however, the little girl begged her to come with them.

So within an hour of reaching home, the three of them changed, made lunch and piled back into Ty's truck. Bouncing over the fields as he headed to a spot he thought would be good, Maddie thought how much fun it would have been to ride their horses. But Darcy hadn't progressed that far yet, and her own skill was novice at best. Though, thanks to Ty's tutelage this week, she wasn't as afraid of the animals as she had once been.

Ty stopped near a group of tall trees, their leafy branches offering shade in the hot Texas sun. In the distance she saw cattle grazing. Several were bunched under another cluster of trees, seeking shade in the sultry afternoon.

Lunch proved delightful. Ty told Darcy about the Hereford cattle on the ranch, how they roamed at will most of the time, but were gathered periodically to move to fresh fields. And at least annually they were gathered for culling, vaccines and to brand the calves.

Despite the shade, the day grew warmer. Replete from a roast beef sandwich and veggie sticks, Maddie felt her eyes closing. She'd rest them a minute, she thought as she lay back on her edge of the blanket.

"Do all the cows have names?" Darcy asked.

He shook his head. "Most don't, that I know of, anyway. They're cattle. You know we sell them for the beef."

She looked perplexed. "What does that mean?"

"They go to a slaughterhouse and become hamburger," he said bluntly.

Her eyes widened and she looked over to the cattle. "They get killed?"

"Where did you think your meat came from?" he asked.

"The grocery store."

He started to say something but realized she looked as if she were about to cry.

"Hey, it's the way things are designed. We grow peaches and apples from trees. Violet grows her tomatoes and pecans. We get fish from streams and the ocean and cattle provides meat." After watching her chase after the piglets, he thought he better not mention bacon and ham.

He'd grown up on a ranch. He couldn't remember when he didn't understand about the purpose of cattle. But Darcy hadn't. He should have watched his words.

He wondered if he would ever make it as a dad. So many pitfalls.

Ty glanced at Maddie. Her eyes were still closed. He could have used her help in this conversation.

A few minutes later Darcy got up and wandered around the shade, spying a tree she thought she could climb. He watched as she scrambled up the lower branches, pausing when she was about six feet from the ground.

The day was warm, but the slight breeze kept it pleasant in the shade. For a few minutes he relaxed and let his thoughts drift. This was what life should be about, a family sharing time together, not going to parties or seeking superficial entertainment, but content to be with each other doing nonspectacular things like lazing around on a quiet Sunday afternoon.

For a moment Ty didn't recognize the feeling—contentment. It came from Darcy—and Maddie—being part of the day. Of knowing he'd done good work this past week. And knowing he was gradually making headway with his unexpected daughter.

He looked over at Maddie. She'd swapped her pretty yellow dress for jeans and a cotton shirt, but somehow they looked more stylish on her than on other women who wore the same attire. Was it the way she carried herself? Or her own innate flair?

She hadn't complained once in his hearing about the differences between the ranch and Fort Worth. He doubted she did around Violet, either, knowing how she didn't put up with whiners.

Checking on Darcy, he smiled when he saw her straddling a large branch, leaning against the tree trunk with a peaceful expression. She found as much contentment here as he did. Could he make her a country girl? She'd asked a couple of times about some computer game she used to play, but he didn't have a computer and so that ended that. He thought she was growing more comfortable around the horses. She sure loved the piglets, chasing after the goat and playing with Nipper when Jack was around.

Maddie shifted and then sat up, her hat falling into her lap. "My one day off and I sleep through it," she grumbled.

He watched her come wide awake. Her cheeks were slightly flushed. Her chocolate-brown eyes sparkled. Her hair fell right into place, brushing against her shoulders, looking like fine silk. His fingers itched to touch it, to see if it was as thick and soft as it looked.

"Only a short nap. Darcy's not even bored yet," he said.

She looked around. "Where is she?"

"Up a tree."

Spotting her, Maddie grinned. "That looks like fun."

"Ever climb one when you were a kid?"

"Never had a tree big enough in the tiny yard we had." She took a deep breath. "I like the smells out here. No exhaust and pollution. Still smells like cattle, though."

Ty felt a surge of yearning—to spend more

Sunday afternoons with her, to be someone she wanted to spend her time with. He half turned from her lest the longing was reflected in his eyes. What happened to his belief she'd turn and run for the city at any moment? That was still a possibility, but somehow he was beginning to doubt she'd do such a thing.

"It's getting late. We should head back," he said gruffly.

"Okay. I thought we could cook steaks on the grill in back of your house. That way all I have to do is the salad and potatoes—I know better than to come between a man and his grill," Maddie said on a teasing note.

He wasn't used to the teasing. He liked it.

"Sounds like a plan. And after dinner, you and Darcy can continue those riding lessons. Today we could have gone farther had we been riding horses rather than in the truck."

"You're on, cowboy. I can't wait to ride like the wind."

Once Darcy was in bed, Maddie told Ty good-night and walked back to the main house. She was hopeful Violet had found some notes or something her mom might have had concerning the picnic. And she wanted to study the folder Sadie had given her. So far she hadn't had a moment to herself.

Not that she minded. The day had been delightful from the inspiring message given by the pastor to the picnic lunch, to dinner in Ty's backyard. For once Darcy had opened up a little, chatting about Rambo and the piglets. She'd even asked Ty a couple of questions, which he answered with as few words as possible.

Maddie teased him once about considering the possibility of expanding his vocabulary. The teasing, amused look he'd given her had sent shivers up her back; she was thrilled to see a lighter side to the man. Which only made her more determined to get to know him better and see if she could coax that side out again.

Once in the main house, she went directly to the office, surprised to find Violet sitting at the desk using the computer.

"Hi," Maddie said. "Where's Landon?"

"He had to go back. How was your day?"

Maddie sat in the one comfortable chair and filled her in on her day.

"Sounds like Ty's making progress," Violet said.

"I guess." Maddie nodded. "Did you find anything on the picnic?"

"Yes, here's the folder Mom had. But guess what else I found today?"

Maddie reached for the folder, opening it to the neat notes Belle had written. She was struck by her neat handwriting. She touched the top paper, tracing her fingertip over the letters. She'd been to see Belle several times, talked to her, urged her to recover. This was her mother's handwriting. She had written these words thinking she'd be coordinating the entire event. How Maddie wished Belle would recover and talk to her. Not only about the past and the choices she'd made, but about today, being involved in the church, running a ranch—no mean feat in this day and age.

"Maddie," Violet said, snapping her out of her reverie.

She looked up. Her sister held out a Bible, white cover, gold edging on the pages.

Maddie smiled. "Is that what you plan to carry when you and Landon get married?" she asked.

Violet shook her head. "I found this in my car when I left church. And the note is identical to yours."

Maddie looked at her in disbelief. "You're kidding."

Violet held out a sheet of paper, creased from being folded in the Bible. "Read it yourself and see."

I am sorry for what I did to you and your family. I hope you and your siblings, especially your twin, can forgive me as I ask the Lord to forgive me.

"Wow, it looks exactly like mine. Wait." Maddie dashed up to her room, found the Bible that had been left at her apartment weeks ago. As she hurried back, she pulled out the sheet of paper from the book. Together the twins looked at the pages side by side. Identical handwriting, identical words.

"Who left it?" Maddie asked softly.

"I have no idea. It was on the seat of the car

when I left church. But I was talking with you and Sadie, and then the Mitchells and Pastor Jeb for a couple of minutes—so anyone at all could have walked by the car and tossed it in. The windows were rolled down."

"When I got mine, I had no idea I had a twin. Obviously, whoever is doing this knows about you, too," Maddie said. "But what does it mean? Who was responsible for separating us when we were young? I don't get it. And how did this person know we were twins before we did? Or where we lived?"

"I have no idea. I've been racking my brain all afternoon trying to figure it out. I was even searching on the internet to see if this Bible came from a special place, but it's a regular Bible, new obviously, but not particularly special in any way."

"Mine is rather nondescript as well." Maddie sighed. "But let's look at that photo again."

Violet had found an old grainy photograph in her mother's hope chest a couple of weeks ago. A picture of a man and woman each holding a toddler and an infant. It had been faded and worn. Landon had taken it to have it enhanced for her. Once done, it clearly showed her mother and Brian standing in front of an older house, each holding identical boys and infant twins. And it had an address she'd traced to Fort Worth.

Violet reached over and plucked it from the desk by the computer keyboard.

"Now that we know the address is in Fort Worth, I think we need to go there and see if we can find out more about our family twenty-five years ago. There might be neighbors still living there who knew them—us."

Maddie stared at her for a moment, then nodded. "I think so, too. Jack needs to come with us. He wants answers as much as we do."

"Maybe more. He was always pestering Mom. Do you think Grayson would be around?" Violet asked.

"Since I've left him half a dozen messages and not heard back, my guess is no. But he'll call as soon as he gets off assignment. I don't want to wait for him, though. Let's go tomorrow."

Chapter Four

Maddie, Violet, Jack and Darcy headed for Fort Worth early the next morning. Since the drive would take five hours, they'd made an early start. Maddie had assured Ty that she could watch his daughter as long as he gave permission for her to go with them. They would not be back before dinner, so he was on his own there.

Jack drove with Violet beside him, and Maddie sat in the back with Darcy.

"Why are we going?" the child asked again. Maddie had explained already at breakfast, but she didn't mind responding again.

"To see if we can discover anything about when we were babies."

She looked at Violet and then Maddie. "You're twins. Ask your mother."

"Belle is our mother," Violet answered. "Did you know she's in the hospital and is in a coma? Do you know what a coma is?"

Darcy shook her head.

"The person's unconscious. Can't wake up," Jack ground out. His sister looked at him with sympathy.

"You can't keep blaming yourself," Violet said gently.

"Why not, Vi? If I hadn't kept pushing for answers, Mom would be fine."

It had been an argument with Jack that had set Belle off on a ride that had ended so tragically. He blamed himself for her injury though he'd hardly been responsible for Belle's horse shying and throwing her off.

"She's still around, you make it sound like she's dead. She'll get better. We've prayed and prayed. I know the Lord answers prayers."

"I know that, too. I also know sometimes He says no," Jack grumbled.

Darcy looked at Maddie. "Is Jack mad?" she whispered.

"No, honey, he's worried about his mom."

The drive took a little under five hours. They had stopped once for a short break, then pushed on. The goal was to get back to the ranch before dark.

Once they reached Fort Worth, Maddie invited them to her apartment. "We can have lunch, regroup and then head for the house."

"I want to go now," Jack said.

"Me, too," Violet said.

"I think a certain little girl needs lunch and I know I do. I hardly ate any breakfast this morning."

Jack glanced at her in the rearview. Maddie knew he held her at a distance. Yet how could he deny she was Violet's twin, thus his sister? Still, they were almost strangers, living in the same house when he was home. Which wasn't often. He and his dog would take off for the far boundary of the ranch to work on that old house and be away for days at a time. He was working through the perceived guilt of his mother's accident. Or trying to tire himself enough to sleep at night.

"Okay, good point. But as soon as we eat, we'll head out," he conceded.

They stopped at a deli for take-out sandwiches and drinks. Maddie had disposed of all perishables at her place when she'd left to visit Colby Ranch.

When the four of them arrived at her condo, she pointed out her parking spot. Violet looked around. "Lots of apartments around here," she said, looking at the high-rise buildings.

"Land's at a premium in Fort Worth, so we build up," Maddie said.

Her apartment was on the third floor. It had a view of the parking garage and another apartment building. But the large windows admitted lots of light, and she'd decorated in a minimalistic style to give the feeling of spaciousness in the limited room.

"Wow, this is cool," Darcy exclaimed as she prowled around the living room while Maddie unpacked the food and took down glasses for the sodas. Darcy might like it, but after her stay on the ranch, Maddie wasn't as thrilled with the apartment as she'd once been. Looking out the windows, she saw glass and concrete instead of rolling hills and end-less vistas. The traffic had been horrendous, and it wasn't even rush hour. She already missed the ranch.

"Oh, I have this print," Violet said, stopping in front of a large print of an old-fashioned street in the rain. "Funny how I didn't notice it the first time I was here."

"Where? I haven't seen it," Maddie said.

"I used to have it in my bedroom. When we painted a couple of years ago, I took it down. I still like it, but I thought the blue tones don't go so well with the yellow I chose for the wall colors." She smiled at her twin.

Maddie smiled back. Another similarity. She loved discovering how alike she and Vi-olet were even though they'd been raised by different parents in different parts of Texas.

"Let's eat and get going," Jack said impa-tiently.

An hour later, he pulled the big truck to a stop before a rundown house in an old neigh-borhood. Stopping the car, he leaned forward to see around Violet. The small house had seen better days.

"The place could use a good paint job and landscaping," he said.

"It's twenty-some years older than the picture," Violet said. "Looking around the neighborhood, it all looks sad and worn. Yet there are a couple of places in pristine condition, like the one across the street."

They all studied that house. Colorful flowers surrounded the walkway. A large maple tree shaded a portion of the front lawn, which was neatly mowed. The lush green grass contrasted sharply to the patchy, weedy yard in front of the old house they'd come to see.

The houses on either side of their old home weren't in much better condition, though an effort had been made to keep the grass short.

"I'll go ask if the current owners know anything," Jack said.

Maddie and Violet got out to stand beside the truck. Darcy had fallen asleep on the short ride from Maddie's place. With the windows rolled down it was as comfortable as it was going to get. Maddie left her door open as well. A slight breeze kept the heat tolerable.

They watched as the door opened and Jack spoke to an older man.

A moment later Jack returned, frowning.

"The house is a rental and the current tenant's only lived here two years. Before that was another family. Who knows how many families have lived here since we did."

"Any neighbors from twenty-five years ago?" Maddie asked.

"Apparently, the woman across the street, Mrs. Patty Earl. She's a widow and keeps to herself, but he said he thinks she's lived on this street the longest."

They all looked at the pristine house and yard.

"Guess we'll try there, then," Maddie said brightly. She couldn't wait to learn more. How wonderful if the woman actually lived here when the Wallace family did—and remembered what had happened to them.

"I'll wait with Darcy, if you two want to go ahead," she said.

"No, we should all go together," Violet said.

"I'll swing the truck into her driveway.

We'll leave the door open and stay on the porch. She'll be okay," Jack said.

Five minutes later they rang the doorbell and waited. Maddie could feel her excitement rise and she exchanged glances with Violet. She could almost feel her twin vibrate with the same anticipation.

The door opened a moment later and a middle-aged woman stared at them. She was tall, thin and her big, bleached blond hairstyle was a testament to an earlier era. Her makeup was just a bit too much, as if she were trying to fight inevitable aging. The slacks and shirt she wore hung on her slight frame. At first her expression was that of wariness, but it gradually changed to suspicion.

"What do you want?" she asked, looking at Violet and Maddie. A frown settled in.

"We believe we used to live in the house across the street, many years ago, and wondered if you lived in the neighborhood at the same time," Jack began.

"What for?" she asked, her expression wary.

"We wanted to know if you knew the Wallace family," Maddie said. "I'm Maddie Wallace."

"Sure I knew your family. If you're Maddie, then you have to be Laurel," she said, looking at Violet. "And you're either Tanner or Grayson. Never had much use for the Wallace family, not after what your mother did to my husband."

Maddie stared at her. "You knew our parents?" She didn't understand the reference to names. Had her mother changed her twin's first name as well as last? And if Grayson kept his name, what happened to Tanner that he became Jack? Maybe the woman was confused.

"I said I did, didn't I? Or at least if you're Isabella's kids. The jury's still out on the father." She started to close her door.

"Wait, please. I'm so confused. Could you explain what you mean?" Maddie asked, holding her hand against the door to prevent the woman from closing it.

"What's to explain? Your family lived here, your mother split, your dad moved away. End of story."

"Our names are different," Violet said. "After all this time, I could understand you not remembering our names. Especially since we were so small."

"I never forgot one thing about Isabella Wallace and her kids," the woman snapped. "After she left, your mother probably changed them. At least she didn't claim the Earl name."

"What does that mean?" Jack asked sharply.

The woman glared at him, then narrowed her eyes as if studying his face. "Don't look much like Joe, but that was the story going around."

"What story?" he asked.

"Who's Joe?" Maddie asked.

"Ask your parents, they know the history."

"Please," Maddie said. "We don't have anyone to turn to. We have to find out about our past. We were separated as far we can figure out when I was an infant. We just recently found each other after twenty-five years apart. We don't know what happened, but now that we've discovered where we used to live, we are trying to piece together the clues to find answers. Did you send us the letter? The Bibles?"

She shook her head. "I don't know about any letters or Bibles. You're the last people I'd want anything to do with."

"Please." Maddie turned, getting more frustrated with the stubborn woman. Her off-the-wall comments made no sense.

Mrs. Earl stared at her for a long moment. Frowning, she shook her head, then reconsidered. "What's to tell? Isabella always wanted her own way. She wanted Brian and got him, but not until after my Joe got her pregnant. At least she didn't try to make a play for him."

"That's not possible," Jack retorted. "Our mother's nothing like that."

"Oh, she was a wild one in high school, let me tell you. Getting pregnant and marrying like that. And two more kids by the time she was eighteen. I know, I was in school with Joe and Brian and Isabella. Can't tell me what's possible and what ain't."

"Then you have firsthand knowledge," Maddie said, trying to placate the woman.

There was so much more going on, she didn't want to alienate her and have her stop talking.

"So you and Joe married and all four of you lived on this street?" Maddie asked.

"Brian's grandma got him that house. Joe and I had to scrimp and save to afford this one. Worth lots more now, but back then it was tough on our starting salaries. At least we stuck together until he died a few years back." She narrowed her eyes. "More than I can say for Isabella cutting out on Brian like that."

"Do you know why Brian and Isabella separated?" Violet asked.

She shrugged, folding her arms across her chest, looking only at Maddie.

"She up and didn't come home one day. A few weeks later, Brian packed up and left. Never saw either again." Her tone indicated she wasn't unhappy about the way things turned out. "At least that got her away from Joe. I didn't want him hankering after her. Or those twin boys—especially later when he and I weren't so blessed."

Jack hit the side of the house in anger and stalked back to the truck. Maddie looked at him, then Violet, who looked as puzzled as she felt.

"So you think maybe Isabella's twin sons were Joe's, not Brian's?" Maddie asked, trying to get the information straight.

From what she'd learned of her biological mother these last weeks, she was a strong Christian whose every action reflected that. Still, one of the great aspects of following the Lord was forgiveness for past sins. One thing she didn't know was when Belle had accepted the Lord.

"I agree with my brother—that's not possible," Violet insisted.

"Joe used to taunt Brian about it, so you figure it out," the woman said. "I'm done talking. You go find your folks and make them tell you what you want to know." She jerked away and slammed the door.

Maddie took a breath. "Maybe there's someone else on the street who would know more," she suggested. Instead of finding out the reason for the split, an entirely new scenario had been dumped on them. Was it possible Grayson was only her half brother? It was so confusing.

"I can't believe what this woman said. My mother would not have done that. Granted, she was young when she had us, but still, that's not like her at all," Violet protested. "She hasn't even dated ever since I can remember. She certainly wouldn't sleep around and then claim one man was the father of her children if another man was."

"We don't know the whole story. Maybe that's why they split," Maddie said.

"Then why did Brian keep Grayson? If he believed Joe was the boys' father, he wouldn't have raised him, would he?" Violet asked.

"Not likely. Actually, Grayson and Dad are lots closer than our father is with either Carter or me," Maddie said. "So that doesn't make sense."

They joined Jack, who was leaning against the front fender, arms crossed over his chest, looking black as a thundercloud.

"Bunch of nonsense," he muttered.

"It sure raises more questions than answers. Do you think she got the names wrong?"

Maddie asked. "It was more than twenty-five years ago and how well do you know people's babies if you're neighbors? And from what she said, they weren't close friends at all."

"Unless you nurse hard feelings for all this time," Violet said, glancing back at the house. "I wish we could find someone else to give another perspective. That woman is seriously angry about it."

Maddie glanced in at Darcy. The child was still lying on the bench seat fast asleep. It was amazing she could sleep through all this.

"Want to ask a few more neighbors if they knew our family?" she asked.

For a moment she thought Jack was going to refuse, but then he inclined his head. "You two go. I'll stay here in case Darcy wakes up."

Fifteen minutes later, Maddie and Violet returned to the car. None of the other neighbors who were home had ever known Brian Wallace or his family.

"Great. Now instead of one question answered, we have a bunch more raised," Maddie lamented as they prepared to return to the ranch.

She expected them to analyze everything on the drive back to the ranch, but the two in the front seat were silent. When Darcy woke a short time after they began driving, Maddie pushed aside her frustration and devoted herself to entertaining the little girl. She'd been good on what had to be, to her, a long and boring day.

They stopped only for a fast-food dinner and ice cream, and then pushed on.

When they reached the ranch, Jack dropped Maddie and Darcy near Ty's cottage and then turned into the drive for the main house.

Ty came out when he heard the truck.

"Hi," Maddie said, surprised at the catch in her heartbeat when she saw him. He was becoming not only familiar, but an important part of her life on the ranch. She tried to draw a calming breath.

"Hi," he replied, nodding to her, and then looked at Darcy. "Have a good day?"

"It was boring," she said, standing a little closer to Maddie.

"It was, wasn't it? You were very good, despite that. Tomorrow we'll do something exciting to make up for today."

"Like what?" she asked, looking up with interest.

"I don't know, I'll figure something out before morning." Maddie hoped she'd come up with something really fun for the little girl.

"Okay."

"Did you get the answers you wanted?" Ty asked.

"I'll tell you later," Maddie said, glancing at Darcy. She knew he probably asked to be polite, but she wanted to tell him all she'd learned. And get another person's opinion on the situation. Jack and Violet were too close to their mother to be objective. However, Mrs. Earl's comments couldn't be ignored.

Maddie had tried her father's phone again on the ride home and been sent straight to voice mail yet again. Which didn't help because the mailbox was still full. Where was he?

She tried to ignore the clamoring of her mind as she joined Ty and Darcy on the walk to the barn. Darcy wanted to ride, but it was too late. Ty promised her he'd quit work early the next day to take her out on a ride.

"Maddie, too?" she asked.

"Sure, Maddie, too."

Terrific. Now she had something else to worry about—leaving the relative safety of the corral and really riding out on the ranch. She hoped she wouldn't make an idiot of herself on a horse with Ty scrutinizing her every move. He already watched her enough to make her self-conscious. She knew he constantly saw her as the fluffy city gal who couldn't do anything around a ranch and yearned for parties and clubs 24/7. Talking herself blue in the face wouldn't work, so her prayer now was he'd see she could cope with things on the ranch and be a help, not a hindrance.

When Darcy was in bed, they moved to the front porch of the cottage. She sat on the bench, while he leaned against the post supporting the overhang. She liked these few minutes each day. Talking about Darcy, discussing the future. She would miss it when she returned to Fort Worth.

"So? Everything not neatly wrapped up?" he surmised.

"Unraveled beyond my wildest imagination, would be more like it." Maddie quickly recounted the afternoon.

"Whoa, you're saying Jack and Violet even had different first names? Couldn't these be middle names and for some reason Belle began to use them?"

"Not likely," Maddie countered. "Especially since we found out a short time ago that Belle Colby isn't even her real name."

"Okay, so she changed her name. Divorced women go back to their maiden names all the time."

"But divorced women usually don't change the children's names—first and last, do they? That's plain odd," Maddie added.

"How did Jack and Violet take it?"

"Jack flared up, of course. I know Violet's as confused as I am. Both stood up for Belle, however. The accusation of her becoming pregnant by someone else was immediately discounted. I have to go with their judgment. They know their mom."

"Your mom, too," Ty reminded her.

"Mmm. I guess."

"Fact."

"Well, I've always thought of Sharla Wallace as my mom. I have all my life. Or at least from whenever I can remember back." She glanced at him. "When do you suppose she and Dad married? And why not tell us she wasn't our mother? Too many questions would result, I guess."

"Check out the county records. Where did they marry?"

"Maybe Appleton? That's where we lived until after her accident. I remember the house there and my room. Not much else. I wish I could reach my dad. Like I said before, he has all the answers."

He turned toward her. "Still MIA, huh?"

She nodded sadly.

"Is he connected with some organization that could track him?" Ty mused.

"No. Not anymore. He used to be but didn't like the bureaucracy. Our home church raises funds and then equips him and off he goes."

"Maybe Pastor Jeb could track him down. He's got contacts all over the state."

Maddie felt a blossom of hope. "That's a great idea. I'll ask in the morning. Speaking of that, did you know the church has a Vacation Bible School starting up next week? Darcy's the perfect age." She looked up at him. "I think it's a good way for her to meet children before school starts. She'll make friends in no time and that'll help get her settled as well. Shall I enroll her?"

He nodded. "If you don't mind taking her and picking her up," he said.

"Of course not. She'll love it."

He gazed at her. "And you, are you settling in? Or did seeing Fort Worth remind you of how much you're missing being home?"

"I'm definitely becoming a country person. I was glad Jack was driving in the city traffic today. How quickly I forgot." She smiled. "I'm getting used to the slower pace of life here."

He looked away. "Not so slow—there's always something to do."

"Different, then, from city life."

"There's that." He pushed away from the post and came to sit beside her on the bench. "There is a movie theater in town."

"I saw it down the block from the café."

"It plays second runs, not first, but if someone hasn't seen a movie he wants to, doesn't matter if it's already played in Dallas or Houston."

"True." She felt her heart flutter again. Was he leading up to asking her out? She thought he didn't like her.

"So this weekend they're playing a Western. Not too many of those around."

"Which is too bad, because they're great movies. Good and evil plainly set out for all to see, and good always triumphs," she said. She waited, but he didn't say anything more.

"I think I'll head for home," she said, rising. Funny how a few weeks ago home was Fort Worth. Now it was her room in the big brick house on a ranch she'd not even known existed all those weeks ago. "See you in the morning."

"In the morning," he said, rising with her.

* * *

Ty watched her walk the short distance to the main house. He wanted to punch something. He'd been that close to asking her out to see the movie. Then the thought of who'd watch Darcy had hit. He wasn't interested in taking Maddie if his daughter tagged along. Was that an awful thought? He loved his child. He wanted to get to know her better, have her trust him, love him in return.

But for one moment, he was willing to hand her off to someone else to watch that evening so he could take Maddie out on a date. How stupid was that?

She'd have probably turned him down anyway—astonished he'd even ask after the way he'd treated her. Why would he think she'd spend any extra time with him? He stared at the darkening sky. Since his divorce and settling in on the Colby Ranch, his life had settled down. Or had it been after he accepted Christ? He still liked to take a woman out sometimes, although he had no interest in the wild parties he'd participated in when on the rodeo circuit.

He'd found joy in learning more about his Lord. He was faithful in attendance at the church, though didn't join in a lot of the extra activities. He had gone to one picnic, and this year he'd take Darcy. She'd love it.

Would Maddie go with them, or stick with Violet and Jack? And Landon. What was the relationship between those two? He wasn't sure. She'd been the reason Landon and Violet met. Yet she loved being with her newfound sister. He'd ask her to go with them and hope she'd say yes.

Time to turn in. Maybe tomorrow he'd be able to issue the invitation to the movies. Maybe he needed to get someone lined up to watch Darcy before he asked.

The next morning as Maddie dressed in her new jeans and a cotton shirt, she thought about the changes she'd experienced over the last few weeks—not the least of which was her wardrobe. The jeans weren't as soft as the slacks she wore at home. They were, however, very practical and wearing them made her feel more like she fit in.

It was awkward being out of step. Everyone on the ranch had been part of it for years. Not only was she a newcomer, she wasn't sure where her place would be if she stayed. Was she going to remain in Grasslands or return to Fort Worth? She'd better make up her mind. If she decided to stay, she needed to find a job beyond this temporary one Ty offered.

She was torn. Her brother Grayson lived in Fort Worth. Her brother Jack lived in Grasslands. Her brother Carter lived wherever the Marines sent him.

She'd known Grayson all her life. She was only getting to know Jack. Either way she went, she'd be hours away from one of her brothers.

As she hurried from the main house to Ty's, Maddie remembered her nervousness that first day. Now it was anticipation that had her rushing over every morning to prepare their breakfast. Watching Darcy proved no hardship. And she found herself daydreaming from time to time about a closer relationship with Ty. She loved the riding lessons. And the quiet time they spent each evening after Darcy went to bed.

And last night she'd thought he was going to ask her out. That popped her bubble. Why hadn't he? Or had she misread everything?

When she entered the kitchen, Ty stood near the counter, watching the coffeepot fill. He looked at her. His dark eyes seemed to lighten a bit. Or was it more of her imagination?

"Good morning," she said, smiling in delight.

"Good morning. Darcy's still asleep. I can grab a bite and take off and you can fix her breakfast later if you want."

"Nope, I'm good with preparing yours and then hers when she wakes. Want eggs and bacon or an omelet?" she asked as she went to the fridge.

He opted for eggs over easy and went to sit at the table, watching her. The silence grew while Maddie felt tongue-tied. She had so many questions to ask, so much she wanted to know. Not only with her own family situation, but about Ty. Here was the perfect opportunity to ask without his daughter around, and yet she didn't know how to begin.

"Want to go to the movies Friday night?" he blurted out.

She spun around, joy flowing through her. He had asked!

"I'd love to," she said, trying not to feel giddy about the invitation.

"I'll see if I can get someone to watch Darcy," he said.

"Okay."

It was a date. Not an outing with his daughter. She turned back to the eggs, her heart feeling lighter than it had in a while. For a short time, she'd focus on the coming date and not the confusion their trip to Fort Worth had added to everything.

It was almost ten o'clock when Maddie and Darcy arrived at the church in town. The white paint gleamed in the sunshine. The tall steeple looked even taller as she approached the church. It was visible from quite a distance. She loved the old building with worn floors and highly polished pews.

Heading to the side where the office was situated, she glanced down the path to the small prayer garden exploding with colorful flowers. It offered a quiet place for meditation and prayer. Her church in Fort Worth was on a busy street. Much as she enjoyed it, there was no quiet space.

She'd explained to Darcy about Vacation Bible School and the little girl had mixed emotions. Never having attended, she didn't know what to expect. And she'd mentioned she'd be the new girl. Maddie wanted her to enjoy herself, but she knew being the new-comer, there would be a settling-in period.

"Will I like it?" Darcy asked yet again.

Maddie was patient in responding. She wanted Darcy to be happy. "I believe so. It'll give you a chance to make new friends. Then you can have a friend to the ranch to visit and you can go to their house for a playdate."

"Like with Sally Skinner," Darcy said.

Maddie quirked a brow. "Who's Sally Skinner?"

"My best friend. She lives in our apartment

building and I can go all by myself to her home, using the elevator."

"That's because you show responsibility and your mother trusted you."

"I miss Mommy," she said in a quiet voice.

Maddie stopped in the walkway to give her a hug. "I know you do, sweetie. But you have your daddy now and he'll take good care of you."

Sadie looked up from the papers on her desk when they entered. She looked almost frightened for a moment, then smiled. "What can I do for you two ladies this morning?"

"I wanted to talk to Pastor Jeb if he's available. And we want to register Darcy for Vacation Bible School," Maddie said, her arm still across Darcy's shoulders.

"The pastor's in his office. If you wish to speak to him privately, I'll register Darcy while you go on in."

The door to the office stood open and Maddie nodded. She smiled at Darcy. "You'll be okay with Sadie, and I'll be right back."

"Okay," Darcy said, going around the desk to stand by Sadie.

"Do you have a minute?" Maddie asked from the doorway to Pastor Jeb's office. It still surprised her that he was so young, only a couple of years older than she was, she guessed. Her pastor in Fort Worth was at least in his sixties. Violet had told her Jeb was a widower. He seemed far too young to have lost someone. His open expression gave her an instant feeling of rapport as he looked up and smiled at her.

"I sure do. Don't tell me, I'll guess—Maddie, right?"

She grinned. "The hair gives me away—I don't wear mine like Violet. But the clothes match."

"Ah, you've discovered my secret. Actually, I was hoping you'd drop by. I like to have a chance to greet and get to know new members, and I haven't had a chance to get to the Colby Ranch lately."

"I'm only visiting right now, so don't know if I'll become a member. I am thinking of staying—if I can find a job." She took the visitor's seat he indicated and sat down.

"I'll keep that in mind if I hear of anything.

How are things coming along for the picnic?" he asked.

"Everything's coming along perfectly. It's been no trouble to call the different committee chairmen and get updates. Everyone I've talked to is excited about the event. I'm looking forward to the picnic myself, and to meeting people in person."

"Glad to hear it. What can I do for you today?"

Maddie told him about her father and his missionary journey through the southern part of the state.

"I'm so anxious to get in touch with him and his voice mailbox is full. He gets so involved with his patients he can forget to eat. Normally it wouldn't matter so much."

"This time's different," Jeb said in his quiet voice.

"You know about our family being split up when we were babies?"

At his nod, she continued. "It's all the questions we have that haven't been answered that are driving me crazy. He could clear things up in a short conversation—if I could only reach him."

"Or if Belle comes out of her coma," he said.

"True. Even better, maybe, since she'd have the answers to some questions that arose recently. Anyway, Ty suggested I ask you if you might have some contacts in other churches who might know something. Dad was going to start in Laredo and move west along the border until El Paso. We don't expect him home until Thanksgiving, but I never anticipated not being able to reach him if I needed him."

"I know some pastors down in that area. I'll make a few calls and see what I can find out," Jeb offered.

"I really appreciate it. Thank you."

"No problem. I know it can be tough when you need to reach someone and can't. Doesn't he check in periodically?"

"Sometimes yes, sometimes no. He gets so caught up in his work. He feels it's important not only to heal those who are sick and can't afford regular medical care, but to feed the soul as well."

Jeb leaned back in his chair, obviously willing to spend as much time as Maddie needed. "Dedicated. We'll see if we can find him. How do you like Grasslands and working for Ty?"

She smiled. "It's growing on me. And watching Darcy is a pleasure. I don't know Ty very well, but he's easy enough to work for." Actually, she wasn't totally sure how she felt about Ty. Better to keep her own counsel for that until she had a better idea of what she felt. And he was easy to work for. Just hard to talk to.

They talked genially for a few more minutes, then Maddie rose to leave.

"I'll call you later with any information I discover," Jeb said, also standing. "I'll walk out with you to see Darcy."

When they entered the main office area, Darcy and Sadie were busy working together on folding the church bulletin.

"Ah, Sadie, you've found a willing helper. Hello," Jeb said with a smile.

Darcy looked up and smiled back. "Hi. She said I could help."

"Very much appreciated," Jeb said.

Maddie watched Sadie when Jeb came closer. The secretary's face flushed and she averted her eyes, focusing solely on the stack of bulletins in front of her as if they were the most important thing in life.

Interesting.

"One more question before we go," Maddie said. "Could you give me the name of a teenager or someone who would like to babysit on Friday night?"

Both Jeb and Sadie looked at her.

"Babysit Darcy?" Sadie asked.

"That's right." Suddenly Maddie wished she'd waited until she'd returned to the ranch and called. With all three of them looking at her in surprise, she felt self-conscious. She suddenly remembered Violet had said Ty didn't date.

"Yes. Ty and I were hoping to go out," she said, feeling more flustered from Darcy's steady gaze than anything.

"I could. I'd love to spend some time with Darcy," Sadie said shyly.

Darcy looked suspicious. "Where are you going?"

"Your father asked me to go to the movies in town. It's not a children's movie or you could come with us."

"If you came to my house, I can show you my new room," Darcy said to Sadie, obviously accepting the fact her father could take Maddie out.

"I'd love to, what time?" Sadie looked at Maddie.

"I'll have to let you know. I'm not sure myself," she replied. She hoped she wasn't overstepping her boundaries, but she was in charge of Darcy, so wanted to make sure she had someone to watch her on Friday.

Jeb left them to discuss Vacation Bible School with Sadie. They chatted a few more minutes, getting information for the morning sessions. Then Maddie and Darcy left.

"Want to eat at the café?" Maddie asked, checking her watch. They'd spent longer at the church than she'd anticipated.

"Yes!" Darcy answered enthusiastically.

It was early afternoon by the time they reached the ranch. Maddie hoped Pastor Jeb would find out something about her father, but she tried not to raise her hopes too high. She was anxious to speak to him, but knew he was so involved in ministering that he forgot all else.

The phone rang almost as soon as they entered Ty's house.

Maddie answered it. It wasn't Pastor Jeb, to her disappointment.

When she hung up, she knew she had to find Ty immediately, hoping he wasn't too far from home.

"I need to talk to your dad," she told Darcy. "Let's see if he's around the barn."

Unlikely. As far as she knew he found every chance he could to ride. Still, it wouldn't hurt to look. She needed to find him as fast as she could.

The barn was deserted except for two horses in stalls.

She went to the main house. Maybe he was meeting with Jack or Violet. But when she reached the house, only the housekeeper, Lupita, was home, vacuuming the front room. Violet had gone into town. Lupita hadn't seen Jack and her husband was working in the truck farm, so he probably hadn't seen Jack, either.

Returning to Ty's house, Maddie settled Darcy in the living room with crayons and paper to draw. She went to the kitchen to try Ty's cell.

"Garland," he answered.

She took a breath. She hated to make this call, but he needed to know as soon as he could.

"Ty, it's Maddie."

"Is something wrong? Darcy?"

"No, well, yes, something's definitely wrong, but Darcy's fine. Ty, I answered your phone earlier and it was Miss Lucas from social services. Darcy's grandparents are home and want her to come live with them. They're threatening legal action."

He was silent a moment. "No."

"No?" she repeated.

"They're not going to take my daughter."

Chapter Five

"I'll be back at the house in half an hour," he said. "I want to hear every word that was said."

"I'll be here." She hung up. Maddie hoped Darcy wasn't going to end up as a pawn in a battle between adults. In her book, Ty should have his daughter. At least for the next ten years to balance out what he'd missed. Darcy was his, though the child knew her grandparents better and sure hadn't warmed up to her father. It was early days, though, and given time she knew Darcy would love Ty.

Only it looked as if maybe he wasn't going to get the time.

It was less than twenty minutes later that Ty strode into the kitchen. Maddie and Darcy were finishing up the cookies and milk they'd had and looked up at his arrival.

"Hi. It seems like I arrived at the right time," he said, looking at the cookies.

Maddie could hear the strain in his voice.

"They're really good. Lupita made them," Darcy said, referring to the ranch's long-time housekeeper.

Maddie tried to read some affection into her tone, but Darcy still had that wary look she so often wore around Ty.

"I'll try them out," he said, his gaze locking with Maddie's.

She could read the frustration. He made the effort, however, to keep things light with Darcy.

When he'd finished, he looked at Darcy.

"Jose needs some help in the barn. Want to help him?"

"Sure," she said with a big grin. "I'll get my hat."

When Ty had taken her to the barn and returned, his expression was grim.

"Tell me everything," he said to Maddie.

"Your case worker at social services called

and asked for you. I explained that I was Darcy's nanny and you were working. She said Brittany's parents had returned from their trip to Africa and learned their daughter had been killed and their granddaughter taken away from Houston. They insist she come live with them." She took a breath. "The social worker said she explained how she found you and that Darcy was with her father. That's when they became quite adamant that Darcy belonged with them and they would be seeking custody."

Ty fisted his hands and looked out the window.

"Can they do that?" Maddie asked. "I mean, they can try, I guess, but you're her father."

"Yeah, let me tell you about me and her grandparents. They have more money than they can spend in a lifetime. I'm a foreman of a ranch in west Texas. I have to work all day." He sighed with frustration. "They're retired, could devote every hour to Darcy. I've saved some money hoping to get my own spread one day, a long court battle will deplete that and then I'll have even less to offer her."

"Those are things. You're her father. Blood ties count. She should stay with you."

"Oh, yeah, and I'm sure you've seen how much she cares about me. Half the time I think she's afraid of me. I would never hurt her!"

"I know that and so does she. I don't think she's afraid of you, more wary. Remember, this is all new to her. Before you showed up a couple of weeks ago, she thought you were dead."

"And I still don't think she's convinced I'm her father," he said.

"Her grandparents have to know."

"Of course. For all I know, they are the ones who kept Brittany from notifying me about Darcy." He scowled. "They were never happy their precious daughter hooked up with a rodeo cowboy."

"What are you going to do?" Maddie asked.

He shook his head. "Stall them, I guess, until Darcy decides she wants to stay here. Surely she has some say in the matter."

"I would think so. I'd suggest we talk to Violet and Landon. Maybe they'll have other ideas," Maddie said.

"Give me the social worker's phone number and I'll call her. See how much time I have. If there's anything to do to avoid court."

"We'll work it out," Maddie said gently.

He raised a brow.

"Hey, I care about her and you. I'm firmly on your side."

"I thought you'd think a city offers more opportunities."

Maddie shot him an exasperated look. "Get over your contempt of cities. They're fine. But so are ranches and woodlands and the beach. It's love of a family that counts, not location."

"You really aren't like Brittany, are you?" he asked huskily.

"Not a bit. Make your call. I'm going to hunt up Violet to see if she's back from town yet. She might have some suggestions. We can call Landon—he knows lots of people and can recommend someone who might know more about this kind of thing."

Ty hung up the phone a half hour later, no more comfortable with what he'd learned than when Maddie had first told him. He should have expected something like this, but he hadn't. This blindsided him. Almost as much as discovering he had an eight-year-old daughter.

The social worker had been totally neutral. The best place for the child would have to be examined if it came to a custody hearing. Judges ruled in the best interest of the child. Could that be quantified without mentioning money? Ty made a good salary. Darcy had her own room in their home and good care with Maddie.

But that was not a long-term solution. What if they questioned his plans for when she was in school? He didn't expect Maddie to remain for the next ten years.

The phone rang. It was Pastor Jeb.

"Maddie said to call this number," the pastor said. "I have some news for her about her father."

Great, Ty thought. He knew she'd been frustrated not hearing from him.

"I'll tell her."

"Everything all right?" Jeb asked. "You're not usually home in the afternoon."

Ty debated telling the pastor, then knew he needed some spiritual support as well as advice. Briefly he described the situation.

"Oh, tough one," Jeb said. "Talk to Stephen Forester. He's the best attorney I know. His office is in the county seat, but he takes a strong interest in anyone who lives in the county."

"I'll do that."

"And before we hang up, we'll take it to the Lord. He'll know what's best," Jeb said gently.

"And what if the Lord doesn't think I'm the best for my daughter?" Ty asked, voicing aloud his greatest fear.

"Then we'll be guided for what *is* best for Darcy. Isn't that what you want?" the pastor asked.

"Yes. Except—I want it to be me," he said in a gruff voice.

"I don't see why it wouldn't be. Let's pray."

Ty felt better when he left the house to go find Maddie. Whatever happened, he'd trust the Lord to know the best solution. And if it was with her grandparents, then he'd still insist on being a part of her life. Darcy was an unexpected blessing he gave thanks for every day. Her living elsewhere wouldn't change that.

"But please, Lord, let her stay with me. I just found her. I can't lose her now," he prayed as he headed for the main house.

Maddie, Violet and Landon were in the office when Lupita showed Ty in. He immediately focused on Maddie.

"Pastor Jeb called. He heard from a church in Blackstone. Your father was there a couple of weeks ago. The pastor's away this week, but the secretary thought your dad was heading west. But she wasn't sure. She's going to check with some others in the church to see if they can remember anything specific."

"Where's Blackstone?" Maddie asked.

"Down near the border," Ty replied.

"Maddie's been telling us about Darcy," Violet said. "Is there anything we can do?"

Ty shook his head. "I don't know. I'm still reeling from the news. How dare they try to come and take my daughter? If I had to guess,

I'd say they were instrumental in keeping all knowledge of Darcy from me."

Landon turned to him. "I have some friends who can help."

"Pastor Jeb recommended Stephen Forester. Ever hear of him?" Ty asked.

"He's good," Landon said with a nod. Then he looked at Violet.

"I've heard of him, he's really good. And local," she confirmed.

"Call him and see what he has to say. You might ask if he can have the venue changed to our county since Darcy resides here. Home turf," Landon suggested. "Easier, too, for you rather than having the hearing in Houston."

"Will they do that?" Ty asked.

"I don't know, but they sure won't if not asked."

"Good advice, thanks."

"So do you want to call that church again to see if the secretary learned anything further?" Violet asked.

"Actually, I'd rather drive to Blackstone to talk to her and to anyone who knew my dad when he was staying there," Maddie said.

"It's a day's drive down and one back," Ty told her.

"Still, talking directly with people who knew him might get more information than a secretary asking around. And how far will she follow up on it? I feel I need to do something," Maddie said restlessly.

Ty cleared his throat. "I'll drive you if you want to go."

"You would?"

"I figure if we're not here for a couple of days, I can't be served with any papers."

Landon chuckled. "Smart man. Take Maddie and go as soon as you speak to the attorney. We'll hold the fort here and let you know if anything or anyone shows up."

Maddie smiled gratefully. "Thanks, Landon." She felt a wave of affection for her longtime friend. Their engagement had been a mistake, which they both acknowledged now. She hoped they would remain friends.

"I'll pack," Maddie said. She turned toward the door and then paused. "Darcy's going with us, right?"

"Of course," Ty said.

"Then I'll pack for her, too. Where will we stay?"

"Let's leave as soon as possible. We'll eat dinner on the road and with any luck be in Blackstone before midnight."

An overnight stay didn't require a lot, so it took Maddie only a few moments to pack. She then ran back downstairs and told Violet and Landon goodbye, hurrying to Ty's place.

Darcy wasn't in the house. Probably still with Jose. She heard Ty in the kitchen talking. Was he still on the phone with the attorney?

She packed enough clothes for Darcy for three days, not forgetting her toothbrush and teddy bear.

When she was ready she went to find Ty.

He hung up as she entered the kitchen.

"Things go okay?" she asked.

"Yeah, fortunately Stephen Forester's assistant knows the Colbys and when I said Violet and Jack would vouch for me, I was put through to the man himself. I explained everything—including our leaving—and he said he'd get right on it. He also told me to tell Violet and Jack that if anything comes to me, it should be sent to him as my attorney. I need to pack and then we can leave."

"I'll tell Violet. Hurry. I don't want to be here if anyone shows up," Maddie said.

He paused a minute. "I appreciate your helping me, Maddie. I don't think I've been as forthcoming as I should have been. The longer I'm around you, the less I see my ex-wife. You are nothing like Brittany and I should have recognized that from the get-go."

She smiled. "Thanks, Ty. That means a lot."

He nodded, as if embarrassed by his statement.

In less than fifteen minutes, Ty got behind the wheel of Maddie's car and the three of them were heading south.

"Where are we going?" Darcy asked again.

Maddie half turned to the backseat to see her. "To Blackstone, it's in south Texas. I've never been there before, so I can't tell you much about it."

Ty looked at her in the rearview mirror. "Might as well get comfortable. We won't get there until after bedtime."

She looked at Maddie for confirmation.

She nodded. "I know it's a long drive, but if we play games or something it'll make the time go by faster. I wish I had a car bingo game. Maybe I could make one."

"What's that?" Ty asked.

"We used it when we took the kids from our church to camp last summer. Instead of letters and numbers, each square has something on it likely to be seen on a trip—you know, like speed-limit signs, traffic signals, railroad-crossing signs. The first person to get all the squares in a row filled in wins. Let me see if I have some blank paper and I'll draw a couple."

Ty glanced at Maddie as she rummaged around in her tote, then glanced back at Darcy. Feeling a wave of love sweep through him, he couldn't bear the thought of her grandparents raising her. He wanted her to know him, know his values, his beliefs. He wanted so much for her, and ached to be a part of her life.

Yet she probably loved her grandparents. He was practically a stranger. Silently he offered a prayer that all things would work

to the glory of the Lord. It was hard sometimes to relinquish all that to the Lord, but he
couldn't do anything on his own. Only with
God's help could he manage. If he lost Darcy,
would that shake his faith? He needed to be
steadfast and know whatever the outcome, it
would be for the best.

"Easier said than done," he muttered.

"What is?" Maddie asked, glancing his way.

"I am trying to put everything at the Lord's
feet and hope He'll handle it the way I want,
or however is best by His will. But I want so
much—" He broke off.

"I know." Maddie reached out and touched
his arm gently. "We'll pray about it, and then
work to the best of our ability to keep things
the way they are."

"Why are we going to Blackstone?" Darcy
asked, looking between Ty and Maddie.

"To see if we can find my father," Maddie explained. She handed back a sheet of
paper and a pencil. "Do you know how to
play bingo?" she asked.

Darcy shook her head.

Ty listened while Maddie patiently explained how the game worked. Once again, he realized how wrong he'd been about her. She reminded him of Brittany—yet she didn't. She had the same flair and sophistication, yet didn't put on an attitude. She was wonderful with Darcy. He remembered every meal they'd shared, the riding lessons, the picnic. The bedtime stories. Sitting on the porch with him after Darcy was in bed, listening to his hopes and dreams for his daughter, offering gentle suggestions about how he could bond them closer together.

She was wonderful with him, too, he thought ruefully.

He glanced over at her. She was so patient with his daughter. Kind and compassionate— exactly like a good woman of faith should be. He was fortunate Violet had suggested her as temporary nanny.

For a moment, Ty wondered if she'd consider the job full-time. It would mean she'd stay beyond September. He'd have someone to talk to, someone to discuss child rearing with. To share delightful moments.

Once again that feeling of contentment

swept through him. A family. They could be a kind of family.

Then he realized the likelihood of that was zilch. Maddie was used to the exciting business world in Fort Worth, not some cattle ranch in west Texas where the highlight of her day would likely be greeting Darcy as she got off the school bus.

"Is your daddy lost?" Darcy asked a few minutes later. She and Maddie had been playing the game, but with little traffic on the road, and fewer signs, neither had completed a row.

"Sort of. I want to talk to him and he's not answering his phone. Pastor Jeb found out where he was, so we're going there to see if we can find where he went."

"Was my daddy lost, too?" she asked.

Maddie looked at him.

Ty cleared his throat. "I was sort of lost. Your mommy didn't know where to find me." He'd give Darcy that. He knew it wasn't her fault Brittany hadn't told him about their daughter.

"But Miss Lucas found you," she said, referring to the social worker.

"She had more resources," Ty said. And the genuine desire to locate him. Which Brittany obviously never had.

"So that was a good thing," Maddie said. "And now you and your daddy will help me find my dad."

"Umm," Darcy said.

Ty could tell she was still processing the entire situation. She'd cried only once that he'd seen over the loss of her mother. She had to be grieving. Brittany was the only parent she'd known all her life. He didn't expect her to get over the loss of her mother anytime soon. He hoped one day he'd be the one she turned to. The one she loved.

"Are you going to get lost again?" she asked.

He met her gaze in the mirror. "Nope, never again. I'll always be right where you expect to find me."

She nodded, seeming satisfied.

Maddie smiled at him and he felt it like a balm. He was as bad as a child, yearning for approval—for her approval.

They stopped for a break and dinner at a small town a few miles off the main highway. Walking around, eating and then using the facilities, the stop didn't take long, and soon they were back on the road. By the time darkness had fallen, Darcy was asleep in the backseat.

Ty pushed on, hoping to arrive in the small town early enough to find good accommodations. He knew Maddie grew more anxious the closer they got. He could feel the tension in the car.

"Want to talk about it?" he asked.

"About what?"

"Whatever has you so on edge."

For a moment he thought she wasn't going to talk, but then she began.

"It's hard not having my father around—especially now." She swallowed hard. "I was astonished to discover I have a twin. That my brother has a twin and neither one of us knew it. At least I assume Grayson doesn't know. And there's no one to talk to about it. No one to give answers, to explain things to us."

"I know that's tough," Ty said.

She nodded. "It is. I so want some sort of explanation. It feels as if we're in a kind of suspended time or something. The more Violet and Jack and I look into things, the more confused it becomes, instead of clearer. I told you about our trip to Fort Worth."

"Which raised even more questions," he replied.

"A lot more. As I mentioned before, according to a very hostile neighbor of the Wallace family, there was rumor that the boys—Jack and Grayson—aren't even my dad's. That made Jack and Violet angry in turn. They say their mom would never do something like that. So we have another question instead of any answers. No one else on the street lived there when our family did."

"And no public records?" he asked.

"Grayson and I have copies of our birth certificates as we needed them for passports a few years back when we went with Dad on one of his mission trips. They state Sharla Wallace is our mother. So what happened there? I can only guess Sharla adopted us.

I never asked because I always thought she was my mom."

"Makes sense since birth certificates are changed in adoptions."

"But Violet and Jack don't have theirs. I think Violet has sent in to get a copy of hers, but until immediately before Belle's accident, they didn't know where to request the birth certificate. They were told they moved to Texas from Washington state and tried to get the records from Washington—to no avail of course, now that we know they were born in Fort Worth like Grayson and I were."

"Did she find the record in Fort Worth?"

"No, actually, she sort of got sidetracked. That was the trip where she and I first met. And she was looking for the birth certificate under Violet Colby. From the neighbor's comments, she started out as Laurel Wallace. I don't know if she's been looking for that birth certificate since we returned." She sighed wistfully. "If only we could get in touch with my dad, he could answer all questions in an instant."

"Or if Belle regains consciousness," Ty said quietly.

"True. I've visited her a few times, you know. She looks so frail lying in the hospital bed with all the tubes hooked up. I'd like to get to know her. I pray every day that she'll wake up and talk to us and not have any lasting brain damage. There are so many unanswered questions. Why did she change not only their last name, but also their first names? Why did she change her own? Why didn't she make any effort over the years to contact Grayson and me?"

"There's still hope. I'm sure once she regains consciousness, she'll be able to answer all the questions."

"I know. I'm trusting God. I don't believe He'd bring me to her and not give me a chance to know her," Maddie said slowly.

"So what would you do to get to know her better—to feel she is your mother?" he queried. "I guess what I'm asking is—what hints can you give me for Darcy? I need to have her want to stay. If she prefers her grandparents, I don't know what I'll do."

"It's different for an adult child. Belle and I would talk, hopefully discover interests we have in common, build a relationship like that. It won't ever be like it would have been had she raised me as she had Violet and Jack." She leaned toward him. "For you and Darcy, talking would be good, too, but at a different level. Find out what her interests are. Do things together. Make happy memories together. Build on what she likes and keep her safe and you'll have a great father-daughter bond."

"I could be out of time," Ty ground out.

"You don't know that. Trust in the Father to do what's best. And if somehow she does go with the grandparents, that doesn't mean it's forever. You could still visit, have her visit, be a part of her life."

He exhaled softly. "That's not always easy."

"No, that's where we have to step up our faith and really hold fast," she said.

Ty mulled over what she was saying. He knew it was true. He was working hard at doing that. Sometimes he faltered, but he resolved to do better. With Christ he could do all things—even deal with this latest development.

When he began to see billboards advertising a national motel chain not too far ahead, he asked her if she wanted to stop there for the night. It was already after midnight and Blackstone was still eighty miles away.

"As good a place as any. We'd reach Blackstone early tomorrow, right?"

"Right. I'm tired and we have no guarantee there's a suitable place in the small town. Stopping here, we'd at least know we have a place to stay for the night."

Ty took care of the registration, saying Maddie could pay him back when they returned home. She appreciated his taking charge. Actually she was warmed to her toes he'd taken off work to drive her. She would have made the trip alone, but being part of a couple was definitely better.

A couple. Sometimes she wondered what would happen in the future if they were closer than now, sharing things friends share—experiences, good times and bad.

Oops, need to focus, she reminded herself.

She was going to find her dad, not daydream about her own future.

Soon Ty bid Maddie and Darcy good-night as they went to the room they were sharing. Ty's room was two doors down from theirs. He promised to wake them in the morning so they could get an early start, then watched as Maddie gave a tired smile and went inside and closed the door.

His room was standard for the motel chain. Tired from driving, but restless with the turn of events, he got ready for bed, but lay there for a long time, staring into the darkness, praying and questioning the Lord. Suddenly, he felt a sweeping sense of contentment. He would trust the Lord in all things.

Right before he fell asleep, he thought of Maddie and her unfailing support. He wished he could count on that forever.

The next morning, Maddie rose before Ty's call. She was already dressed and anxious to get to Blackstone to talk to anyone who might have some clue about where her father was going next. Maybe they could drive to his next stop today and find him. No matter how caught up he was in his mission work, he'd stop to talk to her if she showed up.

After breakfast, they resumed their drive. Arriving in Blackstone shortly after nine, Ty drove straight to the church. The big brick church was right off the main street. Plenty of parking on either side, with discreet signs pointing to the office. Fortunately, the secretary was already there. Mrs. McCaffrey was tall and thin with snow-white hair and a rosy complexion.

"Gracious, I had no idea you would come down here," she said, after introductions were made. "After your pastor called, I asked one of the older members of the church about Dr. Wallace. Pastor Sanchez is away this week at a conference. Our member was asking around. Let me call him and see what he turned up." She invited them to sit in the small reception area while she made her call.

She smiled when she hung up. "Edgar said your father stayed with the Wileys for a few nights. We try to put him up in homes of our congregation. His work is so important, we were lucky to have him here for the days he could spare. Let me call over there."

Maddie could scarcely hold her anticipation as Ty followed the directions the secretary gave to the Wileys' home. The older woman was standing by the door when they drew up in front of the white clapboard house. She smiled and held the screen open as they walked up the path.

"This is a pleasure," she said, smiling warmly at Maddie. "My husband and I so enjoyed having your father stay with us. He wasn't here a lot, but when he was, he told us such interesting stories of what he's done. What a blessing he is. Come in, come in."

"Did he say where he was going next?" Maddie asked after greeting Mrs. Wiley and taking a seat on the edge of a sofa.

"Dear me, he might have, but I wasn't paying attention if he did. I know he talked about a lot of places needing help so desperately, what with the economy and all. Some of our towns along the border are just downright impoverished. And he loves helping the children. I do know he talked about the itinerant

farm workers and how they had such poor opportunities for quality medical care. Maybe
he's gone after some of those as they follow
the harvest."

Maddie asked a few more questions, growing discouraged as Mrs. Wiley was unable
to tell her anything for certain. Finally, she
looked at Ty.

"Why don't you give her your phone number?" Ty suggested with a smile for the older
woman. "If she thinks of anything, she can
call you."

"Oh, it went plumb out of my head, but your
mentioning the phone reminds me. Your father left his cell phone behind. I bet it fell out
of his pocket, as I found it in the sofa cush-
ions about two days after he left. Surely he's
missed it by now, but he's never called to ask
about it. I kept it, thinking he would call and
tell me where to send it. Let me get it for you."
She bustled out of the room.

"Well, that explains why he's not returning
my calls," Maddie said with a sigh. "And either he hasn't missed it, didn't know where
he might have lost it, or is too busy to notice."

"He could have written it off and bought a new one," Ty said.

"Then I think he would have contacted me and Grayson to give us the new number. I'm thinking he hasn't missed it. You don't know how focused he can be."

Mrs. Wiley bustled back in, smiling, holding out the phone.

"I'll tell your father if he calls that I returned his phone to you," she said, handing it to Maddie.

"Thank you. And if he does call asking about the phone, please ask him to call me right away. I really need to talk with him," Maddie said, scribbling her name and phone number on a piece of paper from the small tablet in her tote.

"Oh, I will, I surely will. He's such a wonderful man, so giving and helpful to those who need him most," Mrs. Wiley said.

When they were back in the car, Ty looked at Maddie.

"Now what?"

"I don't know. If he went to help migrant workers, there are only about a gazillion farms where he could be. We could drive around this part of Texas for months and not find him. I was so hoping someone in town would know exactly where he's heading."

"We could try a few towns along the road west of here," Ty suggested.

Maddie stared at her father's phone as if it would give her a clue as to where he'd gone. "No. Thanks for offering. But I don't expect to go chasing all over Texas trying to find him. We tried, and it didn't work out. Thanks for that. He'll call when he calls. Let's find a place to have lunch. Maybe get something at a deli and find a park to eat in before heading home."

The local grocery store provided fresh sandwiches, drinks and cookies. The park in the center of town had playground equipment, picnic tables and lots of benches beneath the shade of century-old oaks.

After they ate, Darcy wanted to play on the swings and slide. She asked Maddie to push her.

"I'll do it. Maddie needs some thinking time," Ty said, rising with Darcy.

Darcy looked at him for a minute then nodded, jumping up to race to the swings.

"You okay?" Ty asked before he followed his daughter.

"I'll be fine. I'm disappointed, that's all," Maddie said. "Go have fun with Darcy."

She watched him walk toward the swing and felt a surge of affection for the man. He seemed lost half the time when dealing with his daughter, but he kept coming back. He was going to be a terrific father for Darcy. He didn't even know how to push her, holding on to the chains at first. But Darcy set him straight and in seconds she was soaring as high as the swing could go. Her laughter rang out and delighted Maddie's heart. She was growing to love the lost little girl.

And her father.

She blinked and caught her breath. She was not falling for a cowboy. She had better sense than that. He'd made it clear from the get-go that she reminded him of his ex-wife and he didn't like her.

Over the weeks she'd been working for him, she knew he had changed some of his opinion. But would he ever see her for exactly who she was, and not a replica of his ex-wife?

What would she do if she fell in love with him? Her home was in Fort Worth. His was in Grasslands. He had to work the ranch. She had no job.

But I could move, she thought. And find a job locally.

And do what?

Not that Ty had given any indication he saw her as more than the nanny he had reluctantly hired to watch his daughter until school started.

And he certainly had enough to deal with when they returned. Until then, however, she could watch him and Darcy and perhaps daydream a bit.

Chapter Six

Ty pushed Darcy high in the swing, delighting in her squeal of laughter.

"Higher!" she insisted.

He pushed harder and she flew up, then back. He was sorry Maddie hadn't found her father, but at least she knew he wasn't deliberately avoiding her—he'd merely left his phone behind. She'd indicated a time or two that he didn't keep in close contact with his children when he was working.

Ty was grateful for the chance to spend more time with Darcy. They'd fallen into a routine at the ranch. She still seemed to be wary around him unless Maddie was with them. In this instance, however, she was acting like the carefree child she should be.

"Can I go on the slide?" she asked a few minutes later.

"Sure." Ty slowed her down and stopped the swing.

"Want me to come, too?" he asked.

She shook her head. "You're too big. Watch me."

"Okay. I'll sit by Maddie, and we'll both watch you."

He ambled over to the bench and sat beside Maddie. "She says I'm too big for the slide."

She laughed. "She's probably right. I love going to the county fair and going down the huge slide in the carnival area. I'd be too big for this one."

He looked at her. "You go on a slide at the county fair?"

"They have these huge ones, as high as a two-story building. It takes a while to climb up all the stairs. Then I use the burlap bag they give everyone and slide down. Never tried it, huh?"

He looked thoughtful for a moment. "I can't remember ever going on a slide. Maybe I did when I was really young, but not since I can remember."

"Then the next time there's a county fair nearby, you should go. And take Darcy, she'd love it."

"You're full of surprises," he murmured.

She grinned at him. For a moment time seemed to stop, then resume. Her smile lit up her face and she was beautiful. He could look at her all day long.

Conscious of the attraction that was growing, he looked away, watching Darcy climb the stairs and slide down the circular slide. She jumped off at the bottom and ran around to climb the stairs again.

"Wonder if I should get a slide for the ranch," he said softly.

"Nope. Part of the specialness of visiting parks is that the equipment is not something children have at home. She's growing to love it at the ranch. Once she can ride competently, she'll be able to explore more and more. If you take her sometimes, she'd be thrilled."

"How about you?" Oops, he shouldn't have let that slip.

"Me?"

"How are you adjusting to living on the ranch?" Once begun, he'd see it through. Plus he was interested in her answer. So far—and it was still early days—she demonstrated none of the frustration and boredom Brittany had. Not that her circumstances were in any way the same. She was still a guest of her sister and brother. Her home was Fort Worth.

"Well—" She looked off into the distance. "Actually, I'm liking it much more than I thought I would when I first learned Violet lived on a ranch. It's quite different from what I'm used to, but it's growing on me." She looked at him with a smile. "And I'm not so afraid of horses, so that's definitely an improvement."

"A healthy regard for horses is good, but you needn't fear any on the ranch."

"That's because you grew up around horses, didn't you?"

He nodded. "My dad was a cowboy on a ranch until they fired him for drinking on the job. He picked up odd jobs after that. Once I started high school, I could get seasonal jobs working ranches in the area. Can't remember when I couldn't ride."

"I'm sorry about your father," she said gently.

Ty shrugged, keeping an eye on Darcy. "It was a long time ago," he said. Not that time blurred all the memories of those days. He'd moved on. But could never fully escape the past.

"I think all children should have a wonderful childhood. One that will help prepare them for their future as an adult, that teaches love and compassion, and faith," she said.

"Yeah, what perfect world is that?"

"Not this one, for sure. But that's what I wish for all kids. You'll give Darcy a happy childhood, teach her right from wrong, and how to give."

"Given the chance, I will." The legal action of his former in-laws weighed heavily on him. He couldn't lose his daughter, he just couldn't!

Ty felt Maddie's hand on his. She squeezed gently.

"Lay it at the Lord's feet, Ty. He is an amazing God. He can do anything. He'll make sure this comes out right."

"Except there's no guarantee that 'right' means she stays with me," he said, his gaze following his daughter's glee in sliding.

"'Right' means according to God's plan. Trust Him."

"I do. I try to." He turned his hand over and clasped hers. Studying their linked hands, he offered a silent prayer that he'd accept whatever came, that he'd trust in the Lord to help him let go of the fear and anguish, and focus on loving his daughter the best he knew how for as long as he could.

They sat in companionable silence for several more minutes, hands together, watching Darcy as she enjoyed the playground.

When she got off the slide the last time and headed their way, Ty released Maddie's hand and stood.

"Ready to get back on the road?" He hated facing what awaited at the ranch, but felt a peace descend that was hard to describe. He was going to trust the Lord and see what happened.

"Yes. Will we get home in time to ride horses?" Darcy asked eagerly.

"Nope. We won't be home until long after dark. We can ride tomorrow," he said.

Maddie stood and gathered their things. "We'll be all rested then and maybe can ride outside of the corral, if your dad thinks we've progressed enough."

"Can we?" Darcy asked, her eyes wide with entreaty.

"If Maddie comes along," he said, giving Maddie a look. "Since she thinks you two are ready."

She laughed. "I asked for that. Sure, I think I'm ready."

They talked about riding for a little while once they were back in the car and heading toward Grasslands. Then Darcy fell silent and when Ty glanced in the rearview mirror, he saw she'd fallen over, asleep.

"If she naps all the way home, she'll be up all night," he said wryly.

"Maybe. But it'll pass the time faster for her. Thanks again for bringing me. I was hoping someone would know where my dad was, but it's not time, I guess."

"You're pretty complaisant about it," he said.

"I could rant and rave, but I still wouldn't know where he is. I trust the Lord to be watching over him."

He glanced at her again. "Sorry we didn't make our date."

She smiled. "This far exceeds a movie. I really appreciate you coming with me—and driving."

"Glad to do it."

Maddie watched Ty as he drove. He focused on the road and for a few minutes she studied him, thinking how much she admired him. He had a way of looking directly at people— honestly and forthrightly. He didn't sugar-coat anything. And she could see he loved his daughter even if she baffled him at times. He should have been a part of her life from her birth. It was sad Darcy had to lose one parent to find the other.

As the afternoon waned, Maddie grew sleepy. She let her eyes drift closed, thinking of all she wanted to do—finish up the planning for the church picnic, see Belle again, seriously consider looking for a job in Grasslands. When she finally succumbed to sleep, she was trying to imagine Ty's reaction when she said she wasn't leaving Grasslands. Would he care, or merely give her his solemn look and wish her the best?

The slowing of the car awakened Maddie. She blinked and looked around. Ty had pulled into the parking lot of a family-style restaurant.

"Stopping for dinner?" she asked.

"It'll be way too late by the time we get home. We'll eat now and when we arrive at the ranch, Darcy'll be ready to go straight to bed."

"Sorry I fell asleep. It had to be boring driving without someone to talk to."

"It gave me time to think. I'm sorry you didn't reach your father."

"He'll call eventually. Either back at that church asking about his phone, or he'll get another one and call me directly. Maybe the lesson to be learned from this is patience."

"Not an easy lesson. I could use some of that myself."

"I think I'll go visit Belle on the weekend. I haven't been since I started working for you. The doctors will call Violet if there's any change, but who knows, something one of us says might be the key to unlocking her silence."

Darcy awoke as Ty pulled into a parking space. "Are we stopping?" she asked, rubbing her eyes.

"We're going to dinner. You hungry?" he murmured, looking at her in the rearview mirror.

"I'm starving."

Maddie smiled. She remembered herself and Grayson telling Rachel they were starving when they were kids. Sometimes it seemed a long time between meals.

They were back on the road an hour later.

Darcy had fallen asleep in the back as the daylight waned. Maddie glanced at her and then Ty.

"Have you spoken to your attorney since we've been gone?" she asked softly.

"No. I gave him my cell number, but told him I'd be in touch when we returned. Unless there was urgent communication needed, I wanted these couple of days. The thing is, if it came to choices, I think Darcy will choose her grandparents. She's still uncomfortable around me."

"More uncertain, I think." Maddie reached over and touched his arm, feeling the warmth beneath her fingertips. "It takes time."

"Which I may not have."

"You're not alone in this, Ty. The Colbys will stand behind you 100 percent."

"How about you?" he asked, flicking her a quick glance.

"Of course. How could you even ask? I personally think she should be with her father. You're doing a good thing here. Anyone could see it."

"I don't have the money the Parkers have. Not to fight the case, nor to provide lavishly for Darcy."

"Kids don't need lavish things, they need attention, to know someone cares. You're showing her that."

He nodded. Maddie could tell how worried he was.

"They've had years to know her," he said. "To her, I'm a stranger." The bleakness in his tone touched her heart. She wished she could say something to comfort him, to reassure him.

"She's getting to know you now. Spend more time with her. Tell her how much she means to you. She can't read minds, you know."

"It's hard to say sometimes," he muttered.

She nodded. Her own father wasn't outspoken about his feelings. She knew he loved her and Grayson and Carter, but he rarely told them. Had whatever happened in the past to split up their family made it difficult for him to express his feelings? Or was that part of the reason for the split? She wished she knew.

When they reached the ranch, Maddie went in with Ty and helped Darcy get ready for bed after Ty carried her in. When she was tucked in, Maddie went to find Ty. "Your turn to tuck her in," she said with a smile. Then her smile faltered. "What?"

He rubbed his hands over his face and shook his head. "Messages from my attorney, the Parkers and their attorney. And a note from Violet that a process server was here yesterday and she took delivery of a summons."

"So first thing in the morning, call your attorney," Maddie urged, her heart aching for him.

"I need to talk to Jack. I might need some time off to fight this."

"Do you want to see if he's home now? I can stay for Darcy," she offered.

"Yeah, might as well get it over with. I'll check in with them after I tell Darcy goodnight."

Maddie went to sit on the porch. The hot August weather held, but after sundown it was balmy enough to enjoy sitting outside. Closing her eyes, she identified all the new sounds she was growing used to—horses shuffling in the corral, blowing their breath loudly sometimes. She heard the distant lowing of cattle. The sound of the goat's bell. No traffic noise, no sirens or horns. It was peaceful. Had she inherited an affinity for this land from the same genes that Violet had? Her sister loved it here. Maddie was growing to love it as well.

She opened her eyes and stared at the starry sky. A short time later, she heard Ty's return.

"All set?" she asked.

"Jack said I can take all the time I need. Which I hope won't be much. It's late. I didn't mean to keep you so long."

"No problem. You drove me to Blackstone, don't forget. Thank you for that. And for being with me." She stood and gave him a smile. When she started to pass, his bleak expression touched her heart.

"Things will be okay, Ty. God promises He's there for us. Trust Him." She reached up and kissed his cheek. "We're all behind you as well." Stepping off the porch, she hurried to the house, wondering if her kiss had been a mistake.

"I'll be over early to fix breakfast," she called back.

He stepped to the edge of the porch. "I appreciate your help, Maddie. I didn't think you'd last two days. I'm glad you stayed."

Her heart skipped a beat and began to race. She turned and tried to see him in the darkness, but he was only slightly silhouetted from the light of the starry sky.

"Good night," she said softly with a wave, then turned and headed for the main house.

His opinion meant a lot to her. She had given her word. He'd realize sooner or later that she stood by it. Now she was sadly counting down the days until he no longer needed her—when Darcy started school. The time was fleeting and there was nothing she could do about it.

Ty watched as Maddie walked quickly away. Her kiss had caught him by surprise. He'd almost given in to impulse and pulled her closer for a real kiss, and then curbed that thought at the last instant. He would like to give her a real kiss. But he wasn't sure where that would lead. Was he feeling more than mere gratitude for her help with his daughter and support for his cause? The last thing he wanted was to alienate her and have Maddie leave before he found another solution to Darcy's care.

Turning to enter the house, he quietly went back to Darcy's bedroom and looked through the open doorway. She looked adorable asleep in the twin bed. Her hair had been brushed and lay around her head on the pillow. The light sheet was enough covers since he didn't have the air-conditioner on.

Thank You, Lord, for this precious child, he prayed. *Let her stay with me, please, Father.*

As it had the night before, a feeling of peace descended. Ty moved to his own room. He was practicing what Maddie had said—trust in the Lord. What other words of wisdom did she have? He had come to the Lord only in the last few years. Was this a test? If so, Ty was going to clamp down on his faith and hold fast.

Once in bed, he reviewed their trip. How he wished they'd found her father. She appeared to take it in stride, but he suspected she was disappointed and frustrated. He would be. If it had been up to him, he would have found the man and made sure he answered all her questions.

Ty almost laughed. Like he was some hero riding in to set things right. He had enough trouble in his own life.

But for a little while he wished he could do something to make Maddie Wallace sit up and take notice.

The next morning Maddie prepared French toast for them, keeping the conversation light. The closer it drew to eight o'clock, the more nervous Ty became. When the phone rang, he snatched it up.

Maddie tried not to listen to the one-sided conversation, especially when he turned his back and hunched over the phone slightly as if to shield himself. Yet she couldn't help hearing the single-word responses.

When he hung up, she looked at him, eyebrows raised in silent question.

"I need to go to Floydada to meet with Stephen. He wants to go over things with me."

He looked so distraught, she wanted to reach out and hug him and offer whatever reassurance she could. Not that it would be much.

"I'll be here with Darcy," she said. "We need to go to the church this morning and review some things with Sadie. I think we're on track for the picnic and am hoping she can catch anything I'm missing."

"I'll let Jack know and then head out," he said. Glancing at the breakfast on the table, he shook his head. "I'll skip it—I'm not hungry."

When Ty had left, Darcy looked at Maddie with wide eyes. "Is he mad at me?"

"Of course not, why would you think that?" Maddie asked, putting French toast on her own plate and going to sit with the child.

"He looked mad."

"He's got a lot of things on his mind. But he's not mad at you at all. He's your father, he loves you."

Darcy ate another bite. "He lets me ride the horses," she mused.

Maddie smiled. "And you're getting good at that."

"He takes us on picnics."

"Yes." She nodded encouragingly.

"I like Jack's dog."

Maddie wondered if that would be enough to keep her with Ty if the judge asked her where she wanted to live. She hoped, for his sake, it would be.

Maddie and Darcy drove into town after nine. She wanted to make sure Sadie would be at the church when they arrived. The parking lot was empty except for two cars.

"Why are we going to church—it's not Sunday," Darcy asked, skipping along beside Maddie as they followed the path to the office.

"I told you, I need to speak to Sadie about the church picnic."

"Oh, yeah. At the lake. I can swim but I don't have my bathing suit. It's at home."

"Honey, your home is on the Colby Ranch now," she reminded her. "I spoke to the social worker and your things are being packed up. I hope they will be delivered soon."

Actually, the conversation had been a bit distressing—Darcy's grandparents were packing up their daughter's apartment and would undoubtedly take all Darcy's things to their place in anticipation of her living with them.

"In time for the picnic?" Darcy asked hopefully.

"I don't know about that. How about we go to the store after we finish here and get you a new suit, then we don't have to worry about your other clothes arriving in time."

"Okay, I want a blue one. Blue is my favorite color."

Sadie and Pastor Jeb were in the office when Maddie and Darcy entered. They had been reviewing the same paper, the pastor leaning over the desk beside Sadie, who was seated in her chair. The exchange appeared sweetly intimate. Both looked up a moment later.

"Good morning," Jeb said with a wide smile of welcome.

"Hi," Sadie said, smiling shyly, glancing at Jeb then back to Maddie and Darcy.

"I brought the folder about the picnic with all my notes. I've spoken to almost everyone and I think we're in good shape," Maddie said. "I wanted to review everything with Sadie so she'd be up to speed."

"Ah, one of our favorite summer events," the pastor said. "No problems, I hope."

"None. Everyone knew what they were doing and were able to educate me when I asked for updates. The only thing I'm not sure about is who's doing the barbecuing. I see where people are bringing meat for the grill, and when Ty took me by the place, I saw several built-in grills but haven't confirmed anyone actually doing the cooking."

"The men usually show up and rotate," Jeb said. "They don't need to be asked. I wouldn't worry about that. We've never had a problem finding volunteers." He smiled at Darcy.

"How are you settling in, young lady?"

"Fine. We're going to buy a bathing suit after we leave here," she said.

"Got to have one for the picnic—everyone goes swimming," Pastor Jeb confirmed.

"Then I'll need one as well," Maddie said. "Unless I go home between now and next weekend to get one there."

"I should have asked as soon as you walked in—how is Belle?"

"The same. We're looking into moving her closer to home. There's not much more the hospital can do until she wakes."

He nodded. "Violet spoke to me about that. We have several closer than Amarillo, which I think would be suitable."

"Tell her we have her in our prayers," Sadie said softly.

"I will," Maddie replied.

"Sadie has taken on the leadership of the prayer chain," Pastor Jeb said with a smile at the secretary.

She blushed and looked down at her desk. "It's my pleasure."

"And we're lucky to have a secretary who wants to become so involved with the church. You're an asset to the congregation, Sadie."

Her face flamed scarlet. Maddie knew she was pleased with the compliment, yet seemed too shy to even acknowledge it. She studied the woman a moment while Jeb talked to Darcy about the forthcoming Vacation Bible School. From the swift glance Sadie gave the pastor, Maddie wondered if the secretary had a secret crush on the minister. Glancing at Jeb she could see why Sadie might. He was a widower, Violet had told her. His reddish hair was cut short, his smile was warm and friendly. And he always had a good word to say about everyone.

She'd have to ask Violet what she thought. It would be nice if two single people fell in love, found common interests and got married.

Unlike her and Ty.

Shocked at the thought, she focused on the pastor and what he was saying to Darcy. She wasn't falling in love with the ranch foreman. They had exactly nothing in common.

Though she did think he was coming around to believing she wasn't totally like his ex-wife—longing for the city scene and loathing the ranch style.

Still, she knew she was too unfamiliar with the seasons of ranching to be of any help to anyone involved in ranching.

She could learn.

Did she want to?

"I'll leave you two to review the picnic,"

Jeb said. "Let me know if you need anything from me."

When he'd left, Maddie took the visitor's chair and opened the folder. "Let me bring you up to date so someone else knows what's going on."

Sadie scooted closer and studied the notes as Maddie reviewed them. Darcy entertained herself for the short time. When they finished, Maddie praised her for being so good. "How about we eat lunch at the coffee shop after we buy your swimsuit?" she said, gathering her notes.

"That'd be fun. Want to come with us?" Darcy invited Sadie.

"Oh, I don't know. It's not lunchtime yet."

"We're going shopping, so you could meet us," Darcy suggested.

"Do join us if you don't have other plans— we can meet at noon," Maddie added. She wanted to get to know this shy woman more. Maybe she could make a new friend at the same time.

"Well, if nothing is happening, I'll come at noon," Sadie said.

"And I can show you my new swimsuit. We're going to get it now!" Darcy said excitedly.

It warmed Maddie's heart to see the young girl so happy and upbeat. It gave her hope that everything would somehow work itself out.

Maddie decided to try another store in town for the swimsuits. The Feed and Grain was fine for Western wear, but she hadn't even noticed swimsuits there. Campbells was the other clothing store in Grasslands and looked like it went on forever toward the back, yet was only as wide as the storefront on Main Street.

The prices were higher than the Feed and Grain, but nothing like Fort Worth prices. When they each found a swimsuit they liked, they also looked for matching cover-ups. It had been Darcy's idea, and Maddie was happy to go along with it.

"That way people will know we're together, because we have look-alike cover-ups," Darcy explained.

"They'll know we're together because we'll be staying together there. No wandering off."

"I wouldn't. But maybe I'll make some new friends."

"You'll know lots of children by the time we have the picnic. It's the Sunday after Vacation Bible School ends, so you'll have met everyone by then."

"Do you think they'll like me?" Darcy asked in a small voice.

Maddie gave her a quick hug. "Of course they will, Darcy. You're a delightful person."

She looked unconvinced, and Maddie wished she knew what she could say to ease her uncertainty.

They arrived at the coffee shop promptly at noon. Sadie was standing out front.

"Hi," she said, smiling at Maddie and then Darcy. She seemed a little out of breath.

"Did you rush over?" Maddie asked. "We would have waited for you."

"Well, I hurried a little. I don't want to take longer than an hour for lunch."

"I know how that goes," Maddie said as she pulled open the door and gestured for Darcy and Sadie to enter. "When I worked at the magazine, it was luxury to even have an hour. There was always so much to do."

"You don't work there anymore?" Sadie asked when they were seated at a booth along the side.

"Laid off. They let fifteen people go the day I got my pink slip. I really miss it. Yet, somehow I wonder if it was the hand of God. I would never have been able to take this much time off to spend with Violet and Jack if I'd still been working. So that part seems like a blessing."

Sadie cleared her throat and glanced at Darcy. "How are Violet and Jack?"

"Fine."

"And their mother?" she asked.

"Belle is still the same. We're planning to move her closer, as I said earlier."

"She's always on the prayer chain," Sadie said softly.

"I appreciate that, and know Violet and Jack do as well. One day I think she'll wake up and be completely healed." She hoped so. There were so many questions she wanted answered—some only a mother could tell her, even if her father explained things.

She still felt odd to think of Belle Colby as her mother.

"The accident was a tragedy," Sadie said. "I know people here in town were shocked. It happened before I came, though, so I didn't know her."

"I'm sure you've heard all the rumors. There's no denying Violet and I are twins. And if you saw my brother Grayson, you'd know he is the exact image of Jack."

"Ready to order?" Gwen asked, coming up to the table. "Hey there, sugar, you want a hamburger and fries?" she asked Darcy.

"Yes, please. And lots of ketchup."

Sadie and Maddie ordered and then Sadie looked at Maddie. "How did your family split up?" she asked.

"I have no idea. None of us does. Belle's unable to answer any questions, of course, and my father's out of touch." Briefly she told Sadie about her father. Ending with, "Ty was so helpful driving me all that way."

"He seems nice. I don't know him very

well. I'm too new to know many of the con-gregation," Sadie said.

"How did you come to Grasslands?" Maddie asked as their lunches were being served. The delay in her response she attributed to Gwen's friendly banter when she brought their iced tea and chocolate milk for Darcy.

But once she'd left, Sadie still didn't answer.

"What brought you to Grasslands?" Maddie asked again.

For a moment, Sadie looked blank. Then she smiled. "I was looking for a quieter place to live than the big city. Spread out a map and closed my eyes and put my finger down."

"Where did you live before?" Maddie asked.

"Dallas," she said quickly.

"I lived in Houston before I came to the ranch," Darcy said.

"I heard that," Sadie said with a sad smile. "We're glad you came here."

"Ty is my dad," Darcy said.

Maddie almost gave a sigh of relief. Was Darcy finally warming to the idea that Ty was her father? She hoped so. So much change in the child's life in such a short time.

"I heard that as well," Sadie said.

"Do you want to see my swimsuit?" Darcy asked, pulling it from the bag.

"I sure do. That's so pretty."

"Do you find it hard to meet people here?" Maddie asked.

"Not working at the church. I was fortunate to get that job right away," Sadie said.

"Pastor Jeb is really great. He helped me find out where my father last visited."

Sadie nodded, dropping her gaze to her salad. "He's wonderful," she said softly.

Once again, Maddie wondered if the secretary had a crush on her boss. Taking in the glasses, baggy clothes and bland colors she wore, Maddie wished she knew Sadie better and could suggest some things to perhaps have Jeb notice her more than just as a secretary.

"Do you still need me to watch Darcy sometime?" Sadie asked a bit later.

"We didn't get our movie night. I don't know if Ty's going to feel like it anytime soon. I'll let you know, if I may?" Maddie said. Their trip south had canceled the planned date. Would he ask her again?

Ty was not back when they returned home. Maddie helped Darcy put away her things, then they went to the barn to check on the animals. Jose rode in and asked if Darcy wanted to help him take care of his horse. Maddie stood in the barn watching the little girl as she carefully brushed the horse's legs. The older cowboy told her all about where he had been and what he'd seen.

When she heard Ty's pickup truck, she looked at Jose. "Will she be okay with you for a little while?"

"Sure. We're getting along fine."

She turned to Ty's little girl. "Darcy, I'll be at your house. When you get done here come right home, okay?"

The child bobbed her head in agreement.

Satisfied, Maddie walked briskly to the house and saw Ty climb out of the truck, holding a file folder.

"How did it go?" she asked when she was closer.

He waited for her and they walked into the house together.

"I know a lot more about legal rights and custodial arrangements than I ever thought I'd know," he said with a weary sigh. "I'd say my chances are about fifty-fifty right now. I think we're getting the venue changed to this county. Which will help a lot with time and expense. It's still going to be a battle. But Forester is cautiously optimistic. The courts usually side with the parents. That being said, the grandparents have known her from birth and have a connection I don't have."

"Hardly your fault."

"That's the part that could go either way. If they say I knew and ignored Darcy, it'd be their word against mine."

"Can't you prove it somehow?" she asked.

"How do I prove it?"

She hadn't a clue, except she knew Ty was as honest as the day was long. His word was his bond. "I think this is where character witnesses come in. Everyone around here knows you're as honest as they come. We might have to ask the entire ranch to testify. That should carry some weight."

He gave a half smile. "Sure be interesting. I can just imagine the faces of Brittany's parents if everyone from the ranch did show up. Wild idea, but not bad. Thanks for the support."

Maddie nodded and kept walking, her heart lighter just being with him.

Chapter Seven

"So what are the next steps?" she asked gently.

"Stephen Forester's in contact with Brittany's parents' attorney, and they are doing as much as they can before the hearing, which they've scheduled for next week. Obviously, we all want this settled as soon as possible."

"Ummm, anything I can do?"

He looked at her. "Pray."

"We could put it on the church prayer chain," she suggested. "I was talking to Sadie earlier about other things and she mentioned Belle is on the prayer chain constantly. I know prayer helps."

"I guess."

She reached out and took his hand. "Don't

guess, Ty, *know.* God hears every word we utter."

"I know… It's just I'm small potatoes compared to the rest of the world."

"Every one of us is as important to the Father as the next person. Trust in Him."

He squeezed her hand gently. "I want to. It's hard. So many things I've counted on have vanished."

"Like?"

"Starting with my mother," he said bitterly. "She abandoned my brother and me years ago. Then Brittany. When life didn't go the way she wanted, she bailed. I hoped to make enough money riding the rodeos to buy my own place, and that didn't happen."

"Don't confuse Darcy with her mother. She's a sweet child who's had a life-altering blow. I can relate to Darcy and losing her mother, I lost mine—" She shook her head. "When I think about it, I lost two mothers. One I don't remember, and the other I've missed ever since she died. It takes time to recover from grief. Not only did she lose her mother, she's living with a stranger in a place totally foreign to where she was raised."

"Sort of like you." He released her hand and brushed a tendril of hair back from her face, looking deep into her eyes. "Thank you for helping with my little girl."

"Glad to do it." She waited a second, hoping for something more.

He dropped his hand and moved into the kitchen, tossing the file onto the counter and going to the refrigerator. "Want something cold to drink?" he asked.

"There's iced tea. I'll take a glass," she said, swallowing her disappointment.

When they both had the cold beverage, he looked around. "Where's Darcy?"

"Out with Jose. He said she wouldn't be a bother."

"Good." He looked at the folder. "Papers to read. Decisions to make."

"Like?" If he wanted to share, she'd be a willing listener. If not, she wouldn't press.

"If I get custody, how often will her grandparents see her. Can she go visit or must they come to the ranch. If I don't get custody, how often do I want to see her, same parameters for visitation. This is my daughter, and the attorney talks about her like she's just a package or something."

"He's probably looking at the law, not the personal aspect. He's good—Violet vouched for him. Pastor Jeb recommended him. You have a lot of people on your side."

"Yeah, and that helps. Apparently, Stephen's been a longtime friend of the Colbys. He highly respects Belle and what she's done with the ranch since old man Crawford died and left it to her."

Maddie felt a small spark of happiness knowing Belle was admired for her accomplishments. She wished she'd recover consciousness. *Her mother.* She felt a wave of longing sweep through her. She hoped she hadn't come this far, discovered Belle was her mother, only to never be able to talk with her. Never know about her life, the struggles and the joys. What she'd thought when Maddie and Violet had been born. What had she wanted for her children when they were infants?

She felt a wave of homesickness for the days when she and Grayson and Carter were still at home, Rachel at the helm and their dad in and out as his studies allowed. Things had seemed much simpler back then.

"I'll go check on Darcy and talk to Jose," Ty said as he set his empty glass down on the counter.

"I'm here if you need me."

He paused a second by the door, then nodded. "Thanks, Maddie."

Ty tilted back on the legs of the chair and studied the star-studded sky. This was his favorite time of day. Work was done. He was pleasantly tired, yet not quite ready for bed. Darcy was asleep and Maddie had returned to the main house. He had the night to himself. He thought about Maddie's comment earlier that Darcy had so many changes in her life, in such a short time. He did, too. Finding out he had a daughter was the most amazing thing that had ever happened to him.

Anger still irritated him that Brittany had kept it from him. Darcy was as much his as hers. His daughter deserved to know him, to learn his values and lifestyle. City living wasn't the only way. He'd known his wife was slightly spoiled when he married her. But he'd truly believed they could make a go of it. That she'd mature enough to see what they had was good, if not as lavish as the lifestyle her parents enjoyed.

More fool, he. She hadn't taken to it at all. But Maddie did.

He frowned. He liked Maddie. Okay, maybe more than liked her. But this was all a vacation to her. Once the novelty wore off, she'd want her gourmet coffee shops, more shopping than Grasslands offered, and the kind of nightlife that could be found into the wee small hours instead of rolling up the sidewalks at six.

For a moment, he almost let himself think of the way things might go if she'd been born and raised on a ranch like Violet. Well, raised on one at least. Violet apparently had been born in Fort Worth, same as Maddie.

Before he could begin to speculate on the Colby family dynamics, he heard a cry.

The front legs of the chair clashed on the deck as he was up and inside in a heartbeat. Darcy was crying. He flipped on the hall light and dashed into her room, leaving the door open so he'd have some light.

She was having a nightmare, thrashing around and crying out.

"Hey, honey, it's okay," he said, scooping her up and sitting on the edge of her bed with her in his lap. "Darcy, wake up, honey. You're okay."

She hiccuped and looked up at him in bewilderment, tears streaking her cheeks.

"You had a bad dream, honey. You're all right," he murmured, rubbing her back gently.

"I dreamed of Mommy. I miss her. I want my mommy," she bawled.

"I know you do. If there was anything I could do to bring her back to you I would, you know that." He rocked her, tightening his arms around her, wishing he could ease her pain. Of course she missed her mother. She was the only parent Darcy had known all her life.

Endless moments crept by and she cried and

cried. He tried soothing her the best he knew how, but it didn't seem to help. He prayed for wisdom to know how to deal with her and wished Maddie was close enough to hear if he yelled. What could he do to ease his daughter's heartache? Only time would heal the wound. And maybe never completely. Darcy would miss her mother all her life.

"Oh, honey, I'm so sorry she's gone." And in that instant, Ty knew he was sorry Brittany was dead. His anger vanished. Brittany had probably done the best she knew how. Her ways weren't his. He knew he would have handled things differently, but in the end, the one who suffered most was Darcy. Had Brittany ever had an inkling she wouldn't be around to see her daughter grown, he knew she would have made arrangements. As he would do if Darcy stayed with him.

"You only get one mother, and I'm sorry she's gone. You know she would have stayed with you if she could have," he said softly, rocking her back and forth.

"I miss her," Darcy said sadly, her sobs slowing.

"It's okay to miss her."

"Do you miss her?"

"I hadn't seen her in a long time, as long as you've been born. But I miss what we had. She was someone I loved very much." Once upon a time.

Could he let himself fall in love again? Her leaving had left a gash in his heart he thought would never heal. Yet as the years had passed, he had found the will to go on. And when he accepted Christ as his Savior, life took on a joy he hadn't expected. This was just a stepping-stone to the next stage of life. One he hoped to enjoy with Darcy.

"Where did you know her?" Darcy asked.

"Oh, we followed the rodeo circuit for a while. Then got married. When I got hurt, she was right there until I was better."

"How did you get hurt?"

"Thrown from a bull."

Darcy pulled back and stared at him. "You rode a bull?"

He nodded.

"That's scary."

"Yeah, it was, actually. And dangerous."

He didn't need to go into all the reasons he'd wanted the big money winning bull-riding events brought. He still had most of it in investments, since he'd never bought that ranch he'd talked about. Another dream that had died when Brittany left.

"Did you and Mommy have a big wedding in the church in Grasslands?" she asked, her tears forgotten.

"No, we had a ceremony in Austin, and your grandmother and grandfather came and friends of your mother and me." It was the first time he'd realized how far apart their worlds had been.

"My grandparents are on a trip to Africa," she said sadly. "I miss them, too."

"They're home now, honey."

Her eyes lit up. "Are they coming to visit?"

Now what? Explain the custody issue? Let her think they couldn't get here for a while? Try to stall?

He took a breath. The truth was the only way. "They want you to come live with them. But I want you to live here. So we're still sorting through things. Once that's decided, they can come to visit." He hoped it would be decided in his favor.

"Where will they sleep? We only have two bedrooms."

Ty clutched at the *we*. Maybe she wouldn't mind staying with him.

"We'll find room. You and I can bunk in the barn if we need to."

She giggled. "With the horses?"

"Sure, well, not exactly with the horses. We'd sleep up in the hay loft. Would you like that?"

"Can Nipper come?" she asked, referring to Jack's dog.

"We'll have to ask Jack, but I'd bet he'd love to camp out in the barn."

She giggled again and Ty hugged her, delighting in her laughter.

"How about we get some hot chocolate before going back to bed?" he asked, lifting her as he stood.

"Okay, can I have marshmallows in mine? Maddie always fixes them that way."

"Sure, if that's the way Maddie does it, we'll do it, too."

She grinned. Her face was blotchy, her eyes puffy, but her grin tugged at his heart. He couldn't lose his little girl.

It was more than an hour later before Ty let himself breathe a sigh of relief. Darcy was sound asleep. He'd checked on her several times after she went back to bed. Their midnight raid on the kitchen had been fun, though he still wished she hadn't had that nightmare.

"Lord, keep her safe," he said softly as he gazed on her from her bedroom doorway. "Let everything work out as You have planned."

Tomorrow he'd ask Jack about being guardian to Darcy if anything happened to him. He needed to know he'd done all he could for his daughter.

He'd known Jack for years. The man was solid, reliable and strong. He'd do his best for Darcy.

If he'd known Maddie longer, if she had a steady job and resources, he might have considered asking her—she and Darcy had definitely bonded.

His prayer was that he'd live a long life and

enjoy all the stages of hers. For a moment he even thought about being a grandfather.

"Your ways are wondrous, Lord," he murmured.

Maddie arrived early the next morning. She was surprised to find the kitchen empty. Usually both Ty and Darcy were both present. Checking her watch she saw it was after six. The coffee wasn't even started.

Preparing breakfast, she wondered if she was going to have to keep it warm for them. Just before the biscuits were done, Ty walked in. She turned to smile at him, her heart catching slightly when she saw him. He looked so strong and self-assured. He was a good man. Surely that would count a lot when the judge was deciding custody.

"Good morning," she said brightly.

"Morning," he replied, heading straight for the coffee she'd made.

"Darcy not up yet?"

"We had a bit of a problem last night. I expect she'll sleep in a bit longer," he said, pouring a cup and then taking a sip of the hot brew.

"What happened?" she asked, pausing as she was about to break an egg into a bowl to make omelets.

He leaned against the counter and looked at the bowl, then glanced at Maddie. "She had a nightmare. About her mother."

"Oh, poor baby," Maddie said with sympathy. "It has to be so hard for her."

"I know. Maybe she would be better off with her grandparents. She cried and cried. I didn't know what to do."

"What did you do?"

"Held her, rocked her, tried to calm her down."

"That's probably the best thing you could have done," Maddie said, wishing she could have been here, too, to help. "I'm a bit surprised she hasn't talked more about her mother. She has to miss her."

He looked at his boots. "I know. We ended up having hot chocolate together and talking about Brittany." It hadn't been as hard as he'd thought, remembering the good times he and Brittany had had. If he could forgive her for leaving him, forgive her for keeping all knowledge of his daughter from him, his memories of the woman he'd once loved would be happy ones.

"Even better. The hardest thing when someone dies is if no one talks about them. I remember Rachel encouraged us to talk about our mother. She had pictures of Mom everywhere and would ask us special memories at every major holiday or birthday. She made it possible for us all to remember her with love." She sighed. "It wasn't always easy. We really missed her for the first few years after her death, but it did get easier."

"You said I should have a picture of Brittany for her. Seems like social services is having her parents clear out her apartment, so all those pictures will go to them. Maybe they'll give some to Darcy. I have a few. I forgot I had them until last night. I'll hunt them up later and give them to Darcy." He never wanted his baby girl to be so sad as she had been last night. If seeing pictures of her mother gave her comfort, he was all for it.

"I'm glad you were there for her last night," Maddie said gently.

He shook his head. "This parenting gig isn't as easy as it looks."

She smiled with amusement. "I don't think it's supposed to be easy. And it's doubly hard when there's only one parent. But with the Lord's help, you can make it."

"Yeah, we'll see. I'm going to talk to Jack today about being her guardian if anything happens to me. I know Brittany didn't expect to die so young. If I die, Darcy will be alone, except for her grandparents, of course. But they aren't all that young. I want someone I respect and trust to watch out for her."

"That's wise. Plan for emergencies and then live like they'll never happen," she replied.

He looked at her. "That movie's still playing in town. Would you like to go out on Friday night?"

Maddie stared at him in surprise.

He wondered what she was thinking. He shouldn't have blurted it out like that. If he had a bit more finesse—

"I'd love to. Thank you for inviting me—

again. We had lunch with Sadie yesterday, and I told her we'd call if we needed her to watch Darcy."

"Great. Then it'll just be you and me. Want to eat dinner before the show, save you making it?"

"I'd like that."

"Good." He drained his coffee cup.

"I'll check on Darcy before we eat. If she's stirring, we can wait, but if she's still out like a light, she'll have to eat later," he said.

Maddie listened to his footsteps as he went back to the bedroom. Ty had asked her out again. Or did it count as a continuation of the first invitation? She couldn't help smiling. Just the two of them. Not that she didn't love Darcy, but it would be wonderful to spend some time with Ty alone.

Well, not completely alone, with other customers at the restaurant and all those attending the movie. She wasn't going to let that stop her enjoyment. She was going on a date with the most fascinating and intriguing man she knew.

Ty left immediately after he ate, saying he

had a lot to do. Maddie cleaned the kitchen, keeping an ear out for Darcy. When she finished, she poured another cup of coffee and went to see if Darcy was still asleep. She was.

Taking her coffee and cell phone out on the front porch, Maddie called Rachel. The longtime housekeeper had always been more than a mere housekeeper. She'd been a surrogate mother to the three motherless children. When Carter had left home, and their dad had chosen full-time mission work, Rachel had declared it was time to retire and she'd moved to Galveston, always wanting to live near the sea. She and Maddie kept in touch by phone and Skype and rarely did a week go by without them catching each other up to date.

"Hello?" she answered right away.

Maddie felt the comfort of her familiar voice. "Hi, Rachel, it's Maddie."

"Hi, honey, how're you doing?"

"I'm doing better than I would have expected, actually, with all things considered."

"Did you and Violet and Jack figure things out?"

"Not yet. In fact, we have a further complication." She told Rachel about going to the old family house in Fort Worth and the accusations the neighbor had made. "Neither Violet nor Jack can believe such a thing about their mother, but with her unable to tell us anything, it just adds to the questions, as you can imagine."

"What does your father say about all this?"

"I still haven't reached him or Grayson." When she thought about her brother, she couldn't believe all she'd learned in the last seven weeks that he was totally unaware of. The revelations would rock his world as it had hers.

"All in the Lord's time, I'm sure," Rachel said. "How's that little girl you're watching?"

"Another complication," Maddie said. "Her grandparents have returned and they are seeking custody. Ty wants her to live with him. So I guess it'll become a court battle with Darcy right in the middle."

"What's a court battle?" Darcy asked from the screen door.

"Oh, oh," Maddie said, looking at the little girl. Her heart sank that she'd inadvertently spilled the beans. "Listen, Rachel, I have to go. Darcy's awake and needs breakfast." And an explanation that could explode everything. Ty was not going to be happy with her.

"Well, this was not enough time to talk. Call me back tonight after your duties are over, however late. In the meantime, I'll pray for you and the whole situation."

Maddie bid her goodbye and shut off the phone, smiling at Darcy as she rose. "Hungry?"

"A little. Did Daddy tell you we had hot chocolate last night?"

Maddie caught her breath when Darcy called Ty *Daddy*. Maybe last night had been a bigger blessing than he knew.

"He did, and that you had a bad nightmare. I'm glad he was there to be with you when you woke up."

"I miss my mommy, but he told me all about her when they were married. And he has some pictures he's gonna show me. And he says it's okay to miss someone when they're gone, and always remember them with love."

"That's exactly right," Maddie said, entering the house and heading for the kitchen.

Darcy was partway through her breakfast before she returned to her question. "What's a court battle?"

"It's slang for a situation being decided in court," Maddie said, hoping she didn't want details.

"And who fights the battle?"

"Mostly attorneys. Men and women who have studied the law for years and know all the rules. They present their cases to a judge and then he decides."

"Is he like a referee?"

Darcy took a sip of juice. "Sort of. What he says goes."

"Where are my grandparents?"

Oh, boy, now the fat would be in the fire.

"They're home in Houston. They came home a couple of days ago," Maddie said, not knowing exactly when they returned, but too soon for Ty and his daughter to completely bond. Given the choice of residences, Maddie expected Darcy would choose the familiar.

"When they come to visit me here, Daddy and I are sleeping in the barn."

Maddie blinked. "Come again?"

Darcy giggled and then resumed eating. "We don't have enough bedrooms, so they can have ours and we'll sleep in the barn—with the horses!"

"Wow, that sounds exciting."

Darcy nodded. "I can't wait! Do you want to come sleep in the barn when we do?" she asked.

"We'll see." She smiled at the child. "Today we need to go up to the main house and talk to Violet. Our mother is being moved to a nursing home closer to us so we can visit her more often."

"I thought your mom was dead," Darcy said, looking puzzled.

"The woman I thought was my mom died when I was little. But then I found out that Belle Colby is my mother. It's hard to get used to."

Darcy studied her face. "Do you have two mothers?"

Maddie sighed. "Apparently so."

"Can I have two mothers?"

"If your dad marries someone, she'd be your new mother, so then you'd have two. But you'll always remember your real mom." At least Maddie hoped she did. She herself had no memories of Belle as her mother. When had the family split? She had to have been an infant—maybe shortly after the picture was taken that Violet had. Grayson didn't remember any other mother beside Sharla.

Once again, the frustration of not knowing what happened rose.

Lord, I'm turning this all over to You. I pray for patience. All will be revealed in Your timing and I need to know that You have everything under control. Please let Dad contact me soon. And keep Belle healing, that she may awaken before long and tell us all we need to know.

When they walked to the main house a short time later, Darcy skipped along beside her. "Can we work in the vegetables today?"

"We'll see if Violet needs us to help. First we need to talk to her. Maybe Jack's dog will be at the house." Nipper was a working dog, but he followed Jack everywhere. If Jack was around today, they'd see his dog.

Violet was in the kitchen with Lupita, sipping a cup of coffee and chatting with the housekeeper as she rolled out dough for a pie.

"Good morning," Violet said when Maddie and Darcy entered.

"What are you making?" Darcy rushed straight to Lupita's side, watching with fascination as she rolled the dough.

"An apple pie. Jack loves those and he needs something to cheer him up these days," Lupita said with a smile for the little girl.

Maddie grabbed a cup of coffee and perched on one of the barstools by the island. "What time did you want to go to Ranchland Manor?" she asked her sister, referring to the place for Belle to be moved to.

"Anytime this morning. I was impressed last time we visited. If we're still impressed, we can sign the papers and arrange transportation for Mom." Violet wrapped her hands around her steaming coffee mug. "The sooner she's here, the more often we can visit."

Maddie nodded pensively. "I'd spend more time with her, but don't know what to say."

"You have enough with watching Darcy. Whenever you can visit, I think she'll know. I hope she knows we're there. The doctor said sometimes comatose patients can hear people talking. So I try to tell her about my day." Her face softened with emotion. "And of course I've told her all about Landon. And you and Grayson. As well as how sorry Jack is about things. It wasn't his fault, but I can't get that through his thick skull."

"Where is Landon? Is he going with us?"

"He's back in Dallas. I can't wait until he moves to Grasslands. This long-distance thing is hard," Violet said.

"When your mom wakes up, you'll get married and you two will be together all the time," Maddie said with a grin. She'd almost had that with Landon, and it had not made her heart beat faster.

Now, if it were with Ty—

Violet grinned. "I can't wait." She tilted her head slightly and looked at Maddie. "She's your mother, too, you know."

Maddie nodded. "I know that. At least intellectually I know it. But I have no memories, no shared experiences, nothing that gives me a feeling of belonging."

"Oh, I wish you did. I thought once you saw her you'd naturally love her as I do. I keep forgetting to you she's a total stranger," Violet said.

They had spent many hours over the last few weeks talking about Belle and Brian, each twin trying to give the other as much information about their parents as they could. But hearing about them wasn't the same as knowing them.

"Same as Dad is to you," Maddie said.

"I really hoped you'd be able to find him when you went to Blackstone."

"I guess it's a test of patience, and I've prayed for more as each day goes by."

Darcy came over to Maddie. "Lupita says I can stay here when you go to the nursing home. Can I?"

Violet nodded. "Great idea. You'd be bored going with us. You don't mind, Lupita?"

"Wouldn't have offered if I minded. You

two girls go on now and get everything set for your mom to come home. Tell her I'm fixing to make her a huge steak with all the trimmings the day she comes back here!"

"I'll tell her. I hope being at Ranchlands will be the closest thing to home we have for now. Maybe even just breathing the same air will have some effect," Violet said.

Maddie hoped something would have an effect and bring Belle back to them.

Ty spent most of the morning taking a tally of the cattle in each section, leaving the one closest to the old house Jack was working on until last. When he spotted the house, he tucked his tally notebook into a pocket and headed for the place.

It had belonged to a neighbor, acquired when the neighbor died and his heirs had sold the property to Belle. Tying his horse to one of the porch rails, he unloosed the saddle and slapped him on the rump as he rounded the horse to step up onto the porch. The sound of a power saw filled the air.

Jack was in one of the first-floor rooms,

cutting a two-by-four that would obviously replace one damaged in the wall where the plaster had been removed. He looked up when Ty entered, cutting the saw off.

"Problem?" he asked, wiping his forehead with his arm.

"No, just wanted to talk for a minute," Ty said, looking around. "You've bitten off a lot here. Need help?"

"It'd probably go faster if I had help, but working keeps me occupied and there's no time limit to finish."

Ty had heard Jack blamed himself for his mother's accident. But he didn't see it. Belle had been a hundred yards or more ahead when her horse shied. Maybe she'd been distracted by their argument, or maybe she'd just fallen. Could happen to anyone.

Ty walked across and looked out the window to the side, studying the view.

"So what's on your mind?" Jack asked.

"I need a favor," Ty said. "A big one."

"Name it," Jack said.

Ty turned. "If something happens to me, would you be guardian for Darcy?"

Jack looked at him a moment, then shook his head. "You sick or something?"

"No. Neither was Brittany. Look at your mom, no telling what could happen in the blink of an eye."

"Yeah, look at my mom. Which is why I wonder if you are certifiable, asking me to watch your daughter. I'm not the man."

"You're the best one I know for the job, and you have Violet to help. I'm hoping to be around long enough to see grandkids, but you never know. And there's not another man I'd trust with the care of Darcy. Could be a moot point, if her grandparents get custody."

Jack stared at him for a long moment. "I never considered being asked as a guardian for anyone—much less a little girl. You know I'll do whatever you need. She's family—like you are. You better stick around until she's all grown up, but yeah, if something happens to you, I'll step in. You know Violet and I will do our best for her."

"Thanks, man. I appreciate it." Ty offered his hand and shook on the deal, feeling a weight lift. He couldn't find a better man than

Jack Colby to take care of his precious daughter if he wasn't around to do the job himself.

The nursing home was situated in the midst of lovely grounds off the highway to Amarillo. The rolling lawn appeared accessible by cement paths meandering through where nurses could easily push wheelchairs to get patients out to the gardens. A profusion of blossoming plants added color and fragrance. The low, brick building looked nestled in the grounds. The serenity of the place was strongly appealing.

Violet, Jack and Maddie had chosen this one as the best option for Belle's continuing care. They were fortunate that Ranchland Manor was equipped to care for comatose patients as well as those well on the way to full recovery from various injuries.

They again toured the facility, had an explanation of the care and treatment Belle would receive when she moved there. It would be perfect, Violet and Maddie agreed. The only thing left now was to make arrangements for her transportation.

On the way out, Maddie took a deep breath. "I love it here. Totally different from the antiseptic hospital feel. And the program they described sounds hopeful, don't you think?"

"I pray every day, several times a day, actually, that Mom will wake up and be back to her normal self. She'll be so surprised to see you. But happy, I know it. I wonder how often she pulled out that picture and looked at it, the one with all of us in it."

"I imagine many times over the years," Maddie said. "With you and Jack, she had a perfect idea of how Grayson and I were growing."

"True, but she had no notion of what you were doing, what was important to you, what made you laugh or cry. You'll love her when you get to know her. She's warm and compassionate and loving. And honorable." She wrung her hands together. "That's why I can't believe what that woman said about her sleeping around before marrying our dad."

"I never picked up a hint that anything like that happened. Of course, I thought Grayson, Carter and I were all Sharla's kids, so who knows what really happened. But I know Dad loves Grayson as much as he loves me and Carter." Maddie glanced at her twin. "If there were any truth to Mrs. Earl's accusations, I think we would have picked up something over the years in Dad's attitude toward Grayson."

"Landon says let it go. That the woman was probably bitterly jealous of Belle in high school and never got over it."

As they were driving back to the ranch, Maddie casually mentioned, "Ty asked me out."

Violet glanced at her. "As in a date?"

"I think so."

She quirked a brow. "You don't know?"

"Yes, it's a date. He's taking me to dinner and a movie. I didn't even know he liked me."

"What's not to like?" her twin asked with a grin.

"He started out thinking I was like his exwife—a city girl through and through and interested in clubs and the fast life in the city. If he only knew the truth." She sighed. "I worked too long to go out very often. I loved my job, but between that, family and church, I didn't date a lot, and certainly didn't go to many clubs."

"So he's seeing you're doing a good job with Darcy and wants to give you a night out," Violet suggested.

"Oh."

"Uh-oh, that sounds disappointed."

"No, if that's all it is, it's fine." She wondered if this was just a reward for a job well done. Was she reading more into it than Ty meant?

"But?" Violet asked perceptively.

"I thought his opinion of me was changing. And actually...I was sort of thinking of looking for something here—a job or something."

"What? That's *fabulous!*" Violet pulled the car off the road and stopped. She reached over and hugged her sister. "That would be the best thing. Fort Worth's too far away."

"I'm just considering it. I'd have to find a job first."

"You already have one with Ty."

"That goes away when school starts. I talked to Sadie yesterday and she found a job almost immediately when she came to Grasslands. So I thought I'd put out some feelers. No magazines are produced here, but I have skills I learned that I can use in a variety of jobs."

"I can't wait to tell Jack...and Mom. They'll be thrilled. You'll find something, I just know it."

"Well, pray about it for me. I haven't begun to look yet and there may be nothing."

"I will pray. I don't know what split us up, but I love that the Lord has brought us back together. Now it looks like we'll be able to spend the rest of our lives catching up."

Maddie didn't bring up Ty's name again. She'd hoped Violet would say something like, "he rarely dates, so it's special he asked you out." Instead, her assessment was probably correct—a thank-you for taking care of Darcy. The salary he was paying her was enough. She didn't need more. Should she back out?

No, she wanted to go with him. She'd have a good time and enjoy every moment they spent together. If that's all they'd have, she'd have a nice memory.

* * *

Ty sat on his horse and quickly counted the cattle in this section. Periodically he took a tally to make sure he didn't need to look for missing cattle. Rustlers weren't as common as they once had been, but in this tight economy there were still those tempted to steal from others to make a quick buck.

That done, he took off his hat, wiped his forehead with his sleeve and reset the hat. It was hot. He'd love to go to the river and take a quick swim. Maybe he'd ride home and get Maddie and Darcy. They both were riding well enough to venture forth away from the barn and corrals. He wasn't sure if he'd have the chance in the future to spontaneously have a swim day with Darcy. He was working hard at trusting in the Lord. Not having years of faith behind him, he nevertheless knew the Lord was looking out for him. A quick prayer and he started for home.

He hoped Maddie and Darcy were there. Maddie had said they were making final arrangements for Belle's move to Grasslands today. If they were still in town, he'd find plenty to do around the homestead. If they returned early enough they could still go swimming.

The farrier was working on reshoeing one of the horses. Two more were tied nearby, awaiting their turn. Ty greeted him, loosened the saddle on his horse and tied him in the shade.

He and Tim Conners chatted for a moment, then he walked to his house. It was empty. Disappointed, he turned to head back to the barn when he heard Darcy's voice talking a mile a minute. He waited on the porch as Maddie and Darcy headed his way from the main house. When his little girl saw him, her face broke into a smile and she ran toward him.

Ty found it hard to swallow. He opened his arms, and she ran right into them, hugging him tightly.

"Lupita let me make a pie with her! I want to have some for dinner and she said we are to come to dinner at the main house and we'll have pie for dessert."

"That sounds good," he said, looking up as

Maddie followed more slowly. For a moment, he wished he could open his arms for her and that she'd rush in and give him a hug, too.

"Dinner with the Colbys?" he asked.

"We're invited. You used to eat there more often before Darcy came, didn't you?"

"Couple of times a week. The rest of the time I usually ate on my own or with the men. What's the occasion?" he asked.

"We're celebrating Belle's return to Grasslands—to Ranchland Manor. She'll be here in two days."

"Any change?"

She shook her head. "Violet called the hospital to arrange everything from that end and her situation's still stable. I wish she'd wake up. There's so much I want to know."

Darcy gazed up at her father. "Belle is Maddie's second mother. Maddie said I could have a second mother if you got married. Are you going to get married so I can have a second mother?" she asked.

That thought caught him unaware. "Well, I haven't given it a lot of thought. The first time I got married it didn't turn out so well."

"I would like to have a second mother. But I miss Mommy."

"You'll miss her for a long time, I expect. She probably misses you," Ty said, holding Darcy's chin in his palm. "She always wanted you to be happy, remember that."

"Okay. Are we going riding?"

"Yes, we are." He looked at Maddie. "It's so hot, I thought we could ride to the river and go swimming. There's a spot where the water moves really slow under some cottonwoods that give shade. Nice this time of day. It's almost too hot to do anything else."

"Sounds like a great plan. Lucky we bought swimsuits for the picnic. We'll change and be ready to go in no time."

Chapter Eight

❧

Swimming had been the perfect suggestion, Ty thought when they were splashing each other in the river. Both Maddie and Darcy had ridden to the spot with no trouble, as if they'd been riding for a long time. Maddie even commented on how much more confident she felt thanks to his pointers, which made him feel about ten feet tall. Darcy could hardly wait to get her jeans off and splash in the river. It was fairly shallow near the bank, tapering down to deeper at the center of the wide river. The current was slow, so no danger of her being carried away.

Maddie plunged in once she stripped down to her dark teal swimsuit. She dove into the water and came up laughing. "This is wonderful," she said, shaking the water from her face, her hair sending drops everywhere.

"I love to swim," Darcy said, swimming out to where Maddie was, holding on to her shoulders and then turning to swim back to Ty.

As the afternoon wore on, they played Marco Polo and then had races. Ty let Darcy win one and she was ecstatic.

To his surprise, he enjoyed being with Maddie as much as with Darcy. She was not fussy about having her hair wet or having her makeup wash off. She laughed and splashed and obviously enjoyed herself.

Suddenly, Ty stopped and listened. Was that thunder? Scanning the skies, he saw thunderclouds in the distance.

"Time to go," he said.

"Oh, I don't want to go," Darcy protested. "We're having fun."

"I know. We'll come again. But I think I heard thunder and if those clouds on the horizon are any indication, we'll have a lightning storm here before long. Too dangerous to be around water if that's the case."

Maddie looked in the direction he'd indicated.

"Okay, let's go," she said, moving directly for shore.

They dried off the best they could with the towels they'd brought, then pulled on their jeans and shirts over damp swimsuits. Maddie kept watching the clouds nervously.

"We'll make it home in plenty of time," Ty reassured her.

She nodded, but continued to look worried.

"Do we have to go?" Darcy asked.

"Tell you what...when we get home, we'll watch a video and have popcorn. How about that?" Maddie said with another anxious glance at the horizon.

By the time they reached the barn, the breeze had kicked up. The clouds were growing larger and darker by the minute. Ty took the reins of all three horses.

"You two go get changed. I'll take care of these fellows and be in when I'm done."

Maddie nodded and headed for the foreman's house, Darcy right beside her.

By the time Ty entered the house a half hour

later, they had changed into dry clothes and were busy popping popcorn. He changed and joined them in the living room as Darcy was going through several movies he didn't even know were there.

"I bought a couple when we were shopping the other day. We were saving them for a rainy day," Maddie explained.

Ty sat at one end of his sofa with Darcy between him and Maddie. The bowl of popcorn sat in Darcy's lap so all could reach it. The cartoon feature had played for only a few minutes when the rumble of thunder could be heard above the sound.

Maddie looked out the window.

"Made it in plenty of time," Ty said, glancing at her. She didn't look reassured.

She looked at the TV and then out the window. A louder clap of thunder sounded and she jumped. Her hands were clenched tightly.

"Maddie, are you okay?" he asked softly.

She glanced at him, her entire body tense. Giving a tight smile, she shrugged. "I don't like thunderstorms."

"Nothing to worry about. If you can hear

the thunder it means the lightning missed you," he said easily.

She nodded, staring out the window again.

When another loud clap sounded, she jumped again.

"Are you scared?" Darcy asked, looking at Maddie.

"Just a little. Always have been." She looked at Ty apologetically. "Sorry."

"Nothing to apologize for. We all have different things that make us uncomfortable," he said.

"Even you?" she asked.

He nodded. "Tell you what, Darcy—you trade places with me and I'll sit in the middle. That way Maddie will have someone solid to hang on to if she needs to."

"Okay."

They made the switch, and no sooner had Ty sat in the middle than a splitting crack of thunder shook the house. Maddie scooted right up against him and he naturally put his arm around her shoulders, pulling her closer. "You're okay," he said, gently as he would to a fractious animal. He rubbed her arm slowly, gradually feeling her relax.

He turned up the sound a bit with the remote. It wouldn't mask the loud claps of thunder, but would minimize the low rumblings.

Maddie couldn't help jumping every time the thunder sounded, yet there was something very comforting about sitting so close to Ty and having his arm around her. She knew the fear of thunder was silly. Yet it was as if it were hardwired into her. Thunder sounded and fear rose.

As the storm moved away she relaxed and began to enjoy the movie. The characters were funny and several times she smiled at Darcy's laughter. The little girl was enjoying it. Lucky her, no fear of thunderstorms.

When the movie ended, the storm had moved on, only the steady rain continued.

"Nice to have some rain and it's already cooler," Ty said, removing his arm from her shoulders.

"Sorry to be such a wimp," she said with a hint of embarrassment. "I've always thought it's because I was in the car when we crashed and my mom was killed. It was storming just like this, only it was at night. I couldn't get out of the seat belt, the rain and thunder scared me and my mom didn't answer."

"Man, that's hard to live through."

"I know, but the thing is, it turns out Violet's scared of them, too—so it might not be from the accident but something that's wired into me."

"A twin thing?" he asked.

"Maybe. Like we both like the color yellow."

"I've noticed you wear it a lot."

"It's my favorite color."

Darcy grabbed a big handful of popcorn. "That was fun, can we watch another one?" she chimed in.

"Since not much work will be done in the rain, I don't see why not," Ty said.

The rest of the afternoon was one of the best Maddie had enjoyed in years. Ty seemed relaxed and at ease around his daughter as never before. And Darcy freely called him Daddy more than once.

Maddie was glad for the change. Hopefully the child would live with him until she was grown. She just wished she could be a part of their lives. At least if she found a job in Grasslands, she'd always be close enough to see them at church or around the ranch, and be able to watch Darcy grow up.

When the second movie ended, it was time for dinner. The rain continued to pour down. Ty dashed out to bring his truck as close to the door as he could. Darcy and Maddie jumped in and they drove the short distance to the main house. Landon and Violet greeted them. Lupita served a delicious roast with all the trimmings and the apple pie she and Darcy had made.

When the blessing had been said and they were eating, Ty asked about Belle.

"She's being transported this weekend. The convalescent home is really nice, clean and efficient. And the best part is we get to visit her without the long drive," Violet said excitedly.

"But no change in her condition, Maddie tells me."

"Not so I can tell, but the doctors say it's

more like she's sleeping. She had REM sleep, and moves sometimes. It's a good sign. Now we wait," Violet said quietly. Landon reached over and gave her hand a quick squeeze.

"The doctors are cautiously optimistic. Which is their way of hedging their prognosis, I think. But I'm clinging to the fact God is the great physician and He can heal anyone. I am holding to faith that the Lord will let her wake up and meet me." Maddie dabbed the corner of her mouth with a napkin. "I can't wait to talk to her, tell her about my life, learn why our family split up—if I don't find out that part from my dad first."

"The uncertainty must drive you nuts. It's driving me crazy," Ty said with a glance to Darcy.

"On Sunday, can I go to Sunday School?" Darcy asked, oblivious to the conversation. "Sadie said it was really fun and there are lots of kids that I'll meet and then go to Vacation Bible School with."

Ty smiled at his daughter. "Sounds like a plan."

"There're adult classes, too," Maddie added.

Ty glanced her way. "You go?"

"I haven't here, but I taught seven-year-olds at my church in Fort Worth. I'd like to see what they have here for adults. Maybe if I find a job and can stay, I'll offer to teach again when the need arises."

"Whoa, what do you mean if you stay?" he asked, staring at her. Violet grinned. Even Landon looked startled.

Maddie looked at each of them. "I've decided with my dad gone so much, and my brothers consumed with their own lives, there's not that much for me in Fort Worth. I'd rather live closer to Violet and Jack. Get to know them better. Be here when Belle awakens. So I've decided to look for work in Grasslands. Or maybe Floydada. It would still be close enough to come to dinner or to spend the day," she said.

Ty put down his fork and stared at her. "I don't know what to say—"

"Guess I caught you off guard," she said with a smile. "Truth is, I really like being here. I'm learning so much about ranching and cattle and how to slow down and savor the day. I like the messages Pastor Jeb gives on Sundays. And once Belle awakens, I'll want to spend a lot of time with her. Nothing's tying me to Fort Worth but the lease on my apartment and it'll be up in a few months."

"I think it's a fabulous idea," Violet said.

"Surprising, I know," Landon said. "But I think you'll like it here, Maddie. I'm looking forward to relocating to Grasslands."

Ty looked at his food.

"I think I'll love living here, with family and friends I hope to make. I feel I've already started with Sadie. I like knowing the Simmonses who own the coffee shop and greet me by name. I know my way around the Feed and Grain."

Ty looked up at her with that comment and gave his slow smile. "That makes you practically a native."

She laughed. "Maybe not, but it's a start."

He didn't say anything more about it, but Maddie caught him glancing at her from time to time as dinner progressed. She wished she could convince him that she knew what she was doing and the change would be welcomed. The Lord knew what He was doing when her job at the magazine ended. Now she trusted Him to lead her to the perfect job locally to enable her to stay in close touch with her twin.

"I loved today," Darcy said as she climbed into her bed some time later. "I got to make a pie, to go riding, go swimming and watch movies. I never got to do that at home. And then I ate with all the grownups at Violet's house."

"This is a different way of life from living in Houston. I'm having to adjust, too. Fort Worth's quite different from Grasslands," Maddie acknowledged. "I think you'll love it as time goes by. Once you've made a lot friends, you can ride together, do things with friends, and maybe your dad'll get you a dog like you asked."

"That would be awesome!" Darcy exclaimed. "I'd take really good care of it."

"Take care of what?" Ty asked, standing in the doorway.

Darcy gazed at her dad. "If I get a dog, I'd

take the bestest care of him," she said earnestly.

"I bet you would. We'll have to see, though."

Maddie knew he was thinking—Darcy's living with him wasn't a sure thing. No promises made until he knew.

When Maddie returned to the main house later, her sister and Landon were together watching a special on TV. She joined them. Smiling at them both, she was reminded yet again of how delighted she was that he and Violet had fallen in love. The only blot on their rosy relationship was Belle's continued coma. She knew Violet wouldn't get married until her mother could be there, so all plans were on hold.

"Your announcement at dinner was a surprise. Are you really going to stay in Grasslands?" Landon asked as she sat on the comfortable recliner next to the sofa.

"I am. If I can find a place to live and a job to support myself."

"You are welcome to stay here," Violet said.

"Thanks. I may have to take you up on it

until my lease ends on the apartment in Fort Worth. I like it here." She paused. "We had a full day today. Fun, too, except for the storm."

"I know what you mean," Violet said. "Scared me, too."

Landon looked from one to the other. "Thunder can't hurt you."

"I know," they said in unison, then grinned at each other.

"Doesn't change the fact it does, though," Maddie said. "Are we going to the nursing home tomorrow?"

"I talked again to the ambulance service before dinner. Mom's scheduled to arrive around eleven. I thought we could go then. If she's late, we can just hang around until they show up."

"Is Jack coming?" Maddie asked.

"I don't know. I told him, but what he'll do is up to him."

"I know he blames himself for her accident, but from what you said, he really wasn't at fault, it was truly an accident. He needs to get over that and be there for your mom when she recovers," Landon said.

"Easier said than done. It's more than just the accident. It's everything we've learned since then. He's having a hard time with the split family, and then the accusations of Patty Earl when we went to the old neighborhood. I wish we could find out more," Violet said.

"Don't we all?" Maddie added under her breath.

"Not much call for the magazine business here," Landon said.

"Maybe she should try the local newspaper. That's still in publishing, and I bet they'd love to have someone with your particular background," Violet suggested.

"I'll check into it next week." Maddie rose. "I'm going to bed. I already told Ty he's on his own with Darcy tomorrow morning since we're going to be at Ranchlands. Wouldn't it be wonderful if Belle wakes up when she arrives? Just knowing she's home might be what she needs."

The next day was clear and cooler after the storm. Maddie prepared breakfast for Darcy and Ty and then joined Violet and Landon for the drive to Ranchlands. Jack had not shown up, and they didn't know if he was coming or not.

Shortly after eleven the ambulance from Amarillo arrived. In short order Belle was transported to the sunny room assigned to her. Once the attendants left and the medical staff had her comfortably situated, Violet leaned over to kiss her mother.

"Hi, Mom. You're back home—well, almost. You're in Grasslands. So much closer that we'll be able to come visit every day." She squeezed her hand. "Lots to tell you since the last time I saw you."

They sat around the bed, talking to Belle, catching her up with all the news—except the comments from Patty Earl.

"You need to come back to us, Mom. We really miss you."

"Me, too," Maddie said, gently caressing Belle's arm. "There's so much for us to talk about. I can't wait."

When a nurse came in to check on Belle, the three of them left. Lunch and then back to the ranch was the plan.

At the coffee shop, they had scarcely begun eating when Violet waved at a man who had just walked in.

"Paul Linder, I want you to meet my sister, Maddie," she said when he stopped by the table. "And my fiancé, Landon Derringer. Paul's the owner and editor in chief at our local paper."

"Pleasure. No denying you're Violet's sister. Once things settle down, maybe we can do a special-interest feature, long-lost family found again," Paul said.

"We'll wait until Mom's better, then we'll get her side," Violet said. "The thing is, Paul, do you know of any work available around town? Maddie's been living in Fort Worth but wants to relocate here. She used to work at a magazine."

"Maybe, depending on your experience. Come see me Monday morning." He fished out a business card and handed it to Maddie. "About ten?"

"Thank you, I'd like that." It would work perfectly, as she could go while Darcy was in Vacation Bible School.

* * *

Maddie dressed with care for her date with Ty. It might only be a thank-you for watching his daughter, but she was going to be at her best. She wore her hair down, brushing against her shoulders. The conditioner she'd used that afternoon gave it gleaming highlights. Subtle makeup to enhance her chocolate-brown eyes and the healthy tan she'd acquired since living on the ranch. The yellow silk blouse she wore was a favorite. The dark brown slacks and high-heeled sandals hadn't been worn in some time. She now knew better what to wear around a ranch. But this was not hanging around the ranch, but dinner and a movie in town.

Even though she loved Darcy, she was looking forward to spending time alone with Ty. Truth was, her feeling of being a buffer between father and daughter was fading. Each day Darcy drew closer to Ty, and he seemed much more comfortable as her dad now.

A few more weeks together and they'd be set forever. She prayed that the custody matter would go in Ty's favor. He needed Darcy as much as she needed him.

Maddie went downstairs just before six. Ty was coming then and she didn't want to keep him waiting. She heard Violet and Landon talking in the living room, but didn't go in. She wanted to hug her anticipation to herself.

When she heard his truck, she let herself out of the house and walked out to meet him as he started up the walk.

"Hi," she said, feeling flustered. She spent a lot of time with him, so why was she suddenly struck with nerves?

"Hi, yourself. You look nice."

"Thanks." She smiled at the compliment. He looked good, too. Dressed up in new jeans, a white shirt and bolo tie.

When they reached his truck, he opened the passenger door for her. She'd ridden in this truck before and immediately noticed the difference. It was spotless. He must have spent a large part of the afternoon cleaning it.

When they were heading to town, she asked, "How did Darcy deal with the fact we were going out without her?"

"She asked if it was a date and said her mom dated a lot. Then she told me about the woman who usually babysat her. She thought it fabulous Sadie had come to watch her. They were already talking about Vacation Bible School when I left. Darcy's looking forward to that."

"You and her mother were divorced a long time. I'm sort of surprised neither of you married again," Maddie said. Obviously, Brittany had dated...why hadn't Ty?

"That marriage cured me of romance," he said. "Don't know why she didn't remarry except maybe she realized she liked the excitement of dating compared to the routine of marriage. Brittany loved living with excitement."

"It'd get tiring after a while, I'd think," Maddie said.

He flicked her a glance. "Yeah."

He drove into the parking lot of Sally's Barbecue a few minutes later. "This okay?"

"Perfect." The barbecue place was down Main Street from the coffee shop. Maddie hadn't been before, but she'd heard Jack raving about it once.

When they were seated, Maddie told Ty about Paul's offer to see her on Monday to discuss different job openings he knew about in Grasslands.

"You're serious about staying, then?" he asked.

"As long as I can get something that will enable me to afford an apartment and all."

"Why not stay with Violet and Jack as you have been doing?"

"I came for a visit, not to move in. It's going to be great living nearby. But they deserve their own home and I deserve mine."

"What if you get a job offer right away?" he asked.

She knew what he was really asking. "I'll tell them I'm available as soon as school starts. That was our deal."

He nodded thoughtfully.

Their food was served and for a few minutes they devoted their attention to enjoying the delicious barbecue ribs, baked beans and cole slaw.

* * *

Ty watched her eat, fascinated she didn't spill a drop of the barbecue sauce on that yellow blouse. She looked amazing tonight. He had quickly grown used to her in jeans with her hair pulled back like Violet wore hers. Tonight it brushed her shoulders and looked as soft as the silky blouse she wore.

When he'd first seen her, his heart dropped. She was too sophisticated for a cowboy like him. Yet she seemed to be enjoying herself. He knew he was.

"So tell me about the truck," she said, looking up with a bright smile.

"That it's so clean?"

"Amazing."

"Darcy and I spent most of the morning getting it in shape. It'll probably stay that way at least through tomorrow when we drive to church."

She laughed. He loved listening to her laugh. He wished he could always bring laughter to her life.

"And did you two have fun?"

"We ended up soaked, as I should have

guessed. But I had her standing in the bed washing the top of the cab, then squirting the bed itself while I cleaned out the inside. Turned out to be fun."

"She's lucky to have you as her dad," Maddie said softly. "Think of the memories you two are making."

"I guess. Doesn't seem like much."

"It's a lot. If you asked me about my childhood, I'd tell you about my brothers, especially Grayson, who always felt he had to watch out for us, and Rachel. She was like a mother to us all. I still call her a couple of times a week. She's wise as well as loving."

He nodded.

"I know my dad loves us. However, I always felt there was a distance between us. Or maybe just an inability to relate. I don't know. But I don't have many memories of him doing things with us kids. Now that I've found out about our family's split, I wonder if that had an impact on how he relates to us. And I'm not sure where Sharla comes into things, except I still think of her as my mom."

"Nice memories there, right?"

"The best. I've been lucky to have her and Rachel, and when Belle wakes up, I'll have another mother to talk to and get advice from."

"You seem sure she's going to do that," he said.

"It's in the Lord's hands. I take all updates the doctors give with an optimistic view. I can't believe I'd find her to lose her before we had a chance to get to know each other."

"I know, I feel that way about Darcy. I'm doing my best to trust in the Lord, but I can't get over worrying about all the money her grandparents have and how little, in comparison, I have."

"It's not about money," she said. "Trust in God. He is able to take care of everything."

"You're right." He was trying to hold on to trust. He wished it came as easily to him as it seemed to with Maddie.

He took a breath, offering up a short prayer that Darcy would remain with him. Then changed the subject. He hadn't brought Maddie out to discuss their families. He wanted to get to know her better.

"Tell me about your job at the magazine," he said.

"I loved it. I was so sorry to lose it, but as well as it's doing, it still feels the loss of advertising money with the economy the way it is." She told him of her responsibilities and the enjoyment she'd derived from doing a good job that was never the same two issues in a row.

She asked Ty about his work on the ranch, and about his plans for the future.

When it was time to leave for the movies, he was sorry to have their conversation end. For once he was almost as talkative as Maddie. She had a way of making him want to share parts of his past with her, as she was sharing with him.

The theater was crowded and they had to stand in line for tickets.

"Want popcorn?" he asked when they entered.

"No, thanks. I'm full from dinner."

Finding two seats together near the center was almost impossible. When he found two near the aisle they nabbed them. Just in time, the lights began to dim and the coming attractions began to play.

Ty reached for her hand, laced their fingers and rested their linked hands on his leg as he watched the movie screen. From the corner of his eye he saw her startled reaction, and then the smile she gave him, tightening her grip slightly.

It was hard to concentrate on the action playing. Most of his attention focused on the woman beside him. Her hand was soft and smaller than his. Her gaze was fixed on the screen, so he glanced at her from time to time, enchanted by her rapt expression as the convoluted plot unfolded.

Another moment of contentment washed through him. He settled in to follow the movie, already hoping she wanted to stop for coffee before they returned to the ranch. He didn't want the evening to end too early.

Maddie tried to watch the movie, but it was almost impossible with Ty holding her hand. Her entire focus was on the warmth of his skin, the calluses she could feel on his palms, and the gentle pattern his thumb traced on the back of her hand. She didn't believe this was a thank-you for watching Darcy.

The minutes ticked by and she wanted to say, "Let's leave the movies and go talk. Tell me what you're thinking. What are you doing holding hands? Do you want a more personal relationship, or am I reading too much into it?"

He'd been pretty adamant over the weeks she'd known him that marriage wasn't for him. With all the changes going on in his life and hers, romance wasn't at the top of her list, either. Yet she was fascinated by him. His slow smile made her insides turn over. His narrowed gaze when she spoke to him had her feeling like she was the only person on the planet.

Worried he'd ask her about the movie later, Maddie did her best to concentrate on the plot, but it couldn't hold her attention as much as Ty did.

When the final credits rolled and the lights came up, Ty released her hand and looked at her.

"Like it?"

"Sure did." She would have liked almost anything with him.

"Want to head to Simmons coffee shop for a cup of coffee and dessert before we head back home?" he asked as they joined the rest of the moviegoers in leaving the theater.

"I'd love to." So he wasn't any more anxious to end their evening than she was.

The coffee shop was surprisingly crowded when they arrived. Others from the theater had the same idea as Ty.

They were shown to a small table near the back. Once they ordered—both apple pie à la mode—Gwen poured coffee and left to get their desserts.

"Does she work all the time?" Maddie asked. "Anytime I come in, she's waiting on customers."

Ty glanced after the owner as she stopped to chat with other customers. He shook his head. "I'm not sure. You're right, she's always here when I come in."

"How are you holding up being away from Darcy?" she asked with a teasing grin.

"What do you mean?"

"I've had friends with babies say the first night out leaving their precious child was almost torture."

"I told Sadie to call me if there were any complications. Since I haven't heard anything, I'm sure they are having a good time together." He checked his watch. "Or did. She should be in bed by now."

"I think Sadie was as excited about watching her as I was about coming tonight," Maddie said. Then she asked, "Any more on the situation with your in-laws?"

"Nothing. A lot of the preliminary work's being done between attorneys, according to Stephen. Anyway, he said he'd let me know when we have a hearing date." He scrubbed a hand across his face. "In a way, I wish it was over. However it goes, at least it wouldn't be hanging over me like this."

"I know. It's the uncertainty that cranks up the frustration level."

"Like you and your family situation—not knowing is the worst," he concurred.

Maddie nodded. "Tell me about riding in rodeos. I've never been to one, though there's a lot of hype when the rodeo comes to Fort Worth."

"I liked it. I was younger then, so getting knocked off didn't matter as much as now."

"Knocked off?"

"I rode broncs and entered a few bull-riding events. I preferred the horses, but the prize money's better on bulls. That cost me."

"That's how you were injured?"

"Violet tell you?" he asked.

"Only that you were injured and that ended your rodeo days."

"And my marriage. Obviously, we weren't the love match I thought we were. Reality has a way of changing things, I guess. At least it was a lesson well learned."

She wished she could say something to ease the disappointment he still felt that his marriage had ended. Could he have found the reason Belle and her father didn't stay married—reality with four children under the age of three was just too much?

But that didn't explain why Belle changed her name and Jack's and Violet's. Was the breakup so bad she wanted nothing to do with the Wallace name? Had she been hiding from her father?

"How's Jack doing? I rarely see him," Maddie said once their pie had been served. The apple pie was perfectly warmed—melting the ice cream, but not too hot to eat.

"He's halfway killing himself working on restoring an old house they acquired a few years back. He's still checking in with Violet about the ranch, but I think the hard work helps him sleep at night."

"Well, if the manual labor helps him stop wallowing in guilt over Belle, then I'm all for it."

"Agreed." He glanced at her. "I saw him the other day. Asked him to be guardian to Darcy if anything happens to me. I also said it might become a moot point if I don't get custody."

"What did he say?"

"He agreed, then told me I better not let anything happen to me."

She laughed. "I think I'm a bit surprised he agreed. He doesn't know anything more about children than you do, does he?"

"No. Still—there isn't another man I'd

rather have charge of my daughter if I'm not there. Jack's honest and a strong Christian. I want her to grow up with that. I wonder sometimes if Brittany and I would have stayed together if we'd trusted in the Lord back then."

"Do you wish you had?" she asked, feeling a bit disappointed. Was he still in love with Brittany?

"I wish I had known the Lord for longer. Maybe I wouldn't have married at all."

"Then you wouldn't have Darcy."

"True, and I'd do anything for her," he said vehemently.

The drive back to the ranch was almost in total silence.

Maddie gazed out at the dark night, thinking about how much she enjoyed the evening—yet they'd done nothing spectacular. She'd never been one for clubs and big parties, preferring evenings with friends or Saturday afternoon barbecues.

When they reached the ranch, Ty stopped by the walkway to the Colby's house. He escorted Maddie to the door. The porch light had been left on for her, though only one light showed from inside.

"Thanks, Ty. I enjoyed myself," she said at the door.

"I did, too, Maddie." He cupped her cheeks in his palms and stared into her eyes. "I hope you'll go out with me again." Then he kissed her.

It was a brief kiss, over before Maddie could even react, except to have her heart race.

"So is this a thank-you for watching Darcy?" she asked when he dropped his hands.

"What are you talking about?"

"Why did you ask me out tonight, as a reward for watching your daughter?" she asked again, seeking clarity.

"I pay you a salary to watch her. This was all for me—and you."

She smiled. "I'm glad. See you in the morning."

Maddie was still smiling as she went up to her room. When she passed Violet's bedroom, the door was open and her twin called out, "How was it?"

She went to the doorway, her eyes sparkling. "Fabulous. We had dinner at Sally's Barbecue, saw some movie and then had dessert at Simmons coffee shop. It was a real date, not a thank-you for watching Darcy."

"Hmm," Violet said with a teasing grin. "Maybe you're the one to soften our lone-wolf cowboy's heart."

Maddie shrugged. Her feelings were too new and tender to expose to anyone—even her sister. "I'm off to bed. Lots to do tomorrow. Good night."

Once in bed, however, she opened her heart in prayer, asking God what His plan for her was. Did she and Ty have a chance to become close—close enough to fall in love and marry?

If she ever married, she wanted it to last a lifetime. He'd already had one divorce and she knew a second would wound him deeply. If they ever contemplated a next step, both of them would have to be very sure.

"If we ask you, Father, perhaps You will be in the midst of our relationship. Let me know what You want for my life. May everything I do or say please You."

Maddie fell asleep thinking about living in Grasslands and sharing her life with Ty and Darcy.

Maddie let herself into Ty's kitchen the next morning. As usual, the coffee was already made. She quickly gathered ingredients for an omelet and began preparing breakfast. Darcy came in before long.

"Good morning, sunshine, how are you today?" Maddie asked her. It was the way Rachel greeted her every morning when she'd been a child.

"I had fun with Sadie. We played checkers and I won sometimes. Sadie's fun. She wants to make lots of friends. She's new like me."

"And me. We all have something in common. Breakfast will be ready soon."

Ty walked in. Maddie caught her breath and smiled.

"Good morning." His look had her heart racing again. "I'll be late getting back tonight," he said as he poured his coffee. "I'm heading to a stock auction in Jack's place. He wants one of the bulls to go on the auction block, but is tied up today and asked me to go."

"Can we go?" Darcy asked.

He looked at Maddie.

"I've never been. It sounds interesting."

"Sure. It's a bunch of animals for sale—horses, bulls, some steers. Other critters, too—sheep, goats."

"Like Nanny?" Darcy asked, referring to the goat that hung around the barn.

Ty nodded. "We need to head out soon, I want to get there before the auction begins at ten."

"We'll be ready," Maddie said, already anticipating spending an entire day with Ty.

Chapter Nine

Maddie had breakfast on the table in less than five minutes. When they finished, Ty said he'd meet them at his truck in twenty minutes; he had to go over things with the men before leaving for the day.

"Do you think we can buy a goat?" Darcy asked.

"I thought you wanted a puppy," Maddie said as she made short work of the dishes.

"I do, but a goat would be something special."

"I tell you what—I'll ask Violet if you can be part owner of Nanny. That way you'll have a goat and we don't have to bring another one on the ranch."

"I like Violet. She's nice. I hope she'll say yes," Darcy said.

"Run and get your hat and we'll go meet your dad."

Maddie needed to run up to the house to get hers as well, but would wait until Darcy joined her.

The phone rang. It was barely eight o'clock. She answered.

"Ty Garland, please," a woman's voice requested.

"He's out now, can I take a message?"

"This is Stephen Forester's office calling. Mr. Forester wanted to speak to him, if possible."

"I'll have him call back in about fifteen minutes, if that's okay."

"We'll await his call."

Darcy ran back into the kitchen, her hat on her head, her teddy bear in her arm. "I'm ready. Teddy wanted to come."

"I bet he's never been to an auction. I need to get my hat and then we need to find your dad. He has a phone call to return before we leave."

Ty didn't like the message when Maddie gave it to him. He headed inside while she and Darcy went to get her hat and wait by the truck. A small stock trailer had been hooked up to the back of his pickup. If they bought the bull, he was obviously bringing him home today.

When he returned, his expression was hard to read. He scooped Darcy up and kissed her cheek. "Ready to go buy some stock?" he asked.

"Yes!"

He opened the passenger door and helped her inside, then Maddie. When they were underway, she looked at him. "News?"

"Later," he said, his gaze straight ahead as he drove down the gravel drive to the highway.

She wanted to know what put that look on his face but, conscious of Darcy right between them, knew it wasn't the time. Later couldn't get here fast enough.

The day was fascinating for Maddie. She and Darcy tagged along with Ty, standing to the side when he dealt with the men selling stock, watching the auction avidly. Maddie was getting a new perspective on Ty as she saw him interact with others. He was obviously well respected. And well-known. He must have been greeted by almost everyone they passed. When he introduced his daughter, everyone made a big fuss over her. Darcy was beaming all afternoon.

He'd introduced Maddie as his friend, not Darcy's nanny. She liked that as well.

On the way back to Grasslands, the bull Jack wanted secured in the stock trailer, Maddie asked if they could possibly stop at the convalescent home. "I want to pop in and see Belle. I wouldn't take long."

"If there's parking for the rig, we could stop for a few minutes," he said.

"Do you want to come in?" she asked.

"I do," said Darcy.

"I'll stay with the rig," Ty said.

The convalescent home was cool when Maddie and Darcy entered a half hour later after Ty pulled the truck and trailer into a shady spot on the outskirts of the parking lot.

They went straight to the nurses' station and asked if they could visit Belle Colby.

The nurse at the station recognized her. "Go right ahead. She had a restful night."

Maddie held Darcy's hand. "Now, don't be upset about the tubes and machines you see. They're feeding her through them since she's still asleep and can't eat."

Belle looked pale and small in the hospital bed. The sides were up and several tubes went from machines on the far side. Her hair was newly washed and spread across her pillow.

"Is she dead?" Darcy whispered.

"No, and you can talk in your normal voice. Hi, Belle. It's Maddie. I've brought Darcy to meet you. She's the little girl I'm watching." Maddie reached out and gently squeezed Belle's hand. "We went to a stock auction today, my first."

"My first, too," Darcy said, standing by the bed and studying the woman lying there. "Is she asleep?"

"Yes. And we want her to wake up soon."

Darcy patted Belle's arm. "I'm going to ask

Violet if I can be part owner of the goat," she told her.

"There's so much for you to catch up on. Wake up soon, okay?" Maddie said. She wished Belle would open her eyes and smile at her. She'd seen pictures at the house. Belle was a beautiful woman who was always caught smiling.

"I'll be back tomorrow," Maddie said. "Now that you are back in Grasslands, we can come visit every day."

There was no response.

Sighing softly, Maddie took Darcy's hand again. "We'll go now."

"Why doesn't she wake up?" Darcy asked as they headed back to the truck.

"She hit her head and it really hurt. So she's coping by sleeping until she's better," Maddie said, trying to make it understandable for Darcy. She knew coma patients sometimes woke up and felt as if they'd been asleep for a day. Others with severe head trauma woke up and remembered nothing. Still others never woke up. She offered up a prayer that Belle would awaken soon as if she'd only fallen asleep for a night.

"How's she doing?" Ty asked when they climbed back into the pickup truck.

"The same. She moves some, makes noises, so that's a good sign, they say. But she is still unconscious. I wish I could do something."

"It's in the Lord's hands," Ty said gently.

"As is everything. You're right. The Lord is in charge. Patience isn't my strongest virtue," she said.

It wasn't until Darcy was in bed that Maddie was alone with Ty. As they'd been doing most evenings, they went to the front porch to sit. He rocked back on the chair, she sat on the bench and leaned against the warmth of the house. The wall held the heat of the day.

"So I assume the attorney had news," she said hesitantly.

"The preliminary hearing will be on Tuesday. The judge had an opening and Forester took it." He rubbed his palms against his jeans. "It's too soon. What if she has to go live with her grandparents? She's only been here a few weeks."

"What if she gets to live here all her life? She'll want to visit them as she gets older, but she's your daughter." She touched his hand. "Keep the faith. The Lord will work everything out. He can do anything."

"I know, but what if working out right means not me?"

"Why would you ever think that, Ty?" she asked. "You're a good man. A Christian who has the respect of everyone we saw today, as well as the men and women on this ranch and in town. You have a great job, a house, money in the bank. Great riches is not the thing custody is decided upon."

"Going against me is that I never even knew I had a daughter until she showed up. I don't own my house, I'm a single father and have no other relatives."

"Two can be a family," she said. "You and Darcy will be a great family."

He stared out over the ranch. Dusk had fallen and in a short time it would be too dark to see much. "Would you go with me?" he asked.

"To the hearing?"

"Yes. I'm to bring Darcy, though I don't think she'll be in the courtroom. But I'd like someone on my side. I'd like it to be you."

"I'd be honored. And I'm sure Jack and Violet and Landon and all the ranch hands and half the town would go in as well."

He shook his head. "It's sort of personal. I know the Colbys would stand by me. And yeah, probably the hands. But I think I just want you."

"Then I shall be there."

"Dressed up?"

She lifted a brow. "Should I?"

"Enough to show there's a good influence on Darcy."

"Superficial, but I'll do it. My most stylish suit and high heels. Is it your intent to distract the judge?"

"Nope, just show the Parkers that Brittany wasn't the only woman in Darcy's life. And you'd be someone they'd recognize as like her."

"I'm not like her," Maddie protested.

"I know that. But you can look like she used

to look, all sophisticated and cosmopolitan. Not like a ranch hand from west Texas."

"I happen to like ranch hands from west Texas," she said softly.

"Let's hope the judge does as well."

Maddie let Ty take Darcy to church the next morning without her. Ever since that night when Darcy had had the nightmare about her mom, she'd been totally comfortable around Ty. Maddie wanted them to have special time together.

She attended with Violet and Landon. She waved at Darcy when they entered, her gaze then moving to Ty. She would never tire of looking at him. He looked happy enough holding his daughter's hand, greeting those he knew. They sat in a pew several behind Maddie. She wished they'd come up to her pew. When Violet nudged her, she looked back to the front.

"I think Sadie's getting braver," her twin whispered. "She's actually sitting in the second row this morning. And the pink blouse she's wearing is pretty."

"We shouldn't talk about her like that. If she has a crush on the pastor, can anything be done to draw his attention?" Maddie whispered back.

"A complete makeover might do the trick, but I don't know if Sadie's ready to go that far. I'm not even sure she knows she's got a crush," Violet responded.

Landon leaned over. "Care to share with the rest of us?"

The twins looked at each other and shook their heads.

"Later," Maddie mouthed, and turned back to the front.

After church, Landon took Violet and Maddie to see Belle.

"Hi, Mom," Violet said when they entered her room. "Pastor Jeb outdid himself today at church. You would have loved it. Landon's here, and Maddie."

The three of them chatted for a while. Violet was constantly at her mother's side, touching her, brushing her hair, linking hands at one point. She believed touch would work as much as hearing her voice.

Before they left, Violet once again asked her mother to wake up. "There's so much you're missing, Mom. We need you. Please, wake up soon."

Maddie felt she was growing to know the woman more and more through Violet's conversations. She yearned for Belle to wake up so she could meet her and Grayson —as soon as he heard the news and could get to Grasslands. Once again she felt isolated from her family, floundering to find answers and hitting brick walls.

On the ride to the ranch, Landon asked again if they'd had any other ideas on who had given them each a Bible with an identical note.

"No, but I think it's some man," Maddie said. "The handwriting's bold with defined downstrokes. I haven't seen anything close in any writing I've seen before. But how did some guy know about our family split before we did?"

"Maybe he knew Mom and Brian when we all lived together in Fort Worth," Violet speculated.

"So why does the note sound as if the person's the reason for the split?"

"Could there have been a love triangle or something?" Landon asked.

Maddie shook her head. "Not with the father I know."

"Or the mother I know," Violet added. "Which makes the rumor Mrs. Earl told us seem very unlikely. Jack's even madder now. He thinks that's the reason Mom would never talk about our father—maybe we didn't have the same one."

"That, I don't believe," Maddie said staunchly. "Dad's an honorable man."

"But we don't know what happened twenty-five years ago," Violet reminded her.

"You're right. If asked before I met you, I'd have adamantly claimed Sharla as my mother. That's another part of the mystery—why didn't Dad ever tell us she wasn't?"

When they reached the ranch, Maddie went upstairs to change. She had to check in with all the committee chairs one last time to make sure everything was a go for next Saturday's picnic. Ty was with Darcy, so she was relieved of duty today.

She had the den to herself as Violet and Landon had gone off together after lunch. When talking to different people, she also had a chance to visit. The long-lost twins story had lost some of its novelty and she chatted amicably with each person. She enjoyed learning more about them and the traditions surrounding the picnic. Really, Sadie should have taken charge of this project—it would have helped her get to know people better.

She was delighted everything was falling into place. Even a stranger could manage this. She looked forward to meeting everyone in person at the picnic. It would be a full and busy day, but sounded like a lot of fun.

While jotting notes, Maddie wondered what Ty and Darcy were doing. She couldn't see his house from this room. They probably had gone out riding, or even swimming. She felt a pang at the thought of them doing things without her. She enjoyed spending time with both of them. Did they miss her?

Lupita looked in a short time later.

"Violet said they would eat out. Jack is still at the other house, so I wasn't planning a dinner tonight, but I can prepare you something."

Sunday was usually her day off and Maddie was touched she thought about her.

"I'll be fine. I might join Ty and Darcy." The perfect excuse. Not that she needed one. She was supposed to be fixing their meals. They'd agreed to let Sunday be Maddie's day of rest, but she could still help out. Maybe they'd grill out.

Before wrapping things up, she ran upstairs to get her own laptop, which had her résumé on it. She studied it a bit, tweaked it slightly and then printed off a couple of copies. She would give one to Paul Linder tomorrow at her interview, and have the other handy, just in case.

It was almost five when she walked over to Ty's house. Knocking on the door, she opened it and called out. No one was home.

She went into the kitchen to check on supplies for dinner and soon had hamburger patties made, a salad and was thawing buns.

Darcy came in the back door and smiled broadly when she saw Maddie.

"Hi! We went riding. I'm getting good. I wanted to go swimming, but we didn't wear our swimsuits," she said, running across the room and hugging Maddie. "We missed you. Why did you have to stay away today?"

"I had things to do for the church picnic. We want that to go well, right?" Maddie said, giving her a hug and looking up as Ty entered.

He took in the preparation and smiled. Her heart flipped over. She released Darcy and turned back to the counter. "I thought we could grill burgers tonight, suit you?"

"Sure does. I didn't expect it, however."

"Oh, I didn't think. Maybe you and Darcy want family time alone," she said turning back to face him.

"Nope. She's right—we missed you on our ride. Get everything set for the picnic?"

"There's so little left to do. The only thing I'm worried about is who's going to cook the tri-tips, but Pastor Jeb assures me men step up and it's always taken care of."

"True. I wouldn't worry about that aspect.

What time do we need to be there?" He placed his hat on the hook near the door and ran his fingers through his hair as he crossed the room to stand beside her, looking at the salad and the buns.

"I need to be there early. It officially starts at eleven but I thought I'd get there at least by ten."

"Earlier, I'd think. Let's plan to get there at nine-thirty. We'll get good parking that way, too. I assume you have things to take."

"Yes—food, folding tables, fly nets. Violet assures me they always take those things and they're all together ready to be loaded. You don't have to go that early."

"Sure we do." He looked at her, his dark eyes holding hers.

Feeling slightly flustered, she smiled. "Thanks, I appreciate it."

"What else did you do today?" he asked.

Chatting as they prepared dinner gave Maddie an insight into how being married would be. She loved discussing what each had done since they'd last seen each other. Darcy chipped in and the feeling of family pervaded.

Ty did a masterful job grilling the hamburgers and they enjoyed eating on the folding table out on the minuscule patio, which sat in shade thanks to where it was situated by the house.

"We have ice cream for dessert," Maddie said. She had brought some from the main house complete with chocolate syrup and chopped pecans from Violet's orchard.

Maddie glanced at Ty and Darcy. "Tomorrow Vacation Bible School starts," she reminded them.

"I know. Sadie told me all she's learned since she's been here. Did you know she just moved here a few weeks ago?"

"Yes, I did. I also know how fast she found a job. I hope I have as much success," Maddie said, licking the last drop of chocolate from her spoon. She put it in the bowl and looked up to meet Ty's eyes.

"Tomorrow will be a big day for both of you," he said.

She nodded.

"But you'll have to miss the end of Tuesday's Bible School," he said. "We have to be in Floydada by two."

"What for?" Darcy asked.

"A hearing."

She frowned. "I can hear."

Maddie smiled. "A different kind of hearing, honey." She looked at Ty. How much should they explain?

He drew a deep breath. "We'll meet with a judge and he'll decide where you're going to live," he said.

Looking perplexed, Darcy glanced at Maddie. "Don't I live here?"

Maddie nodded. "Yes, you do."

"And both Maddie and I are happy you do. But your grandparents also want you to live with them," Ty explained.

Maddie held her breath. Darcy looked back and forth and then wrinkled her nose.

"They don't have goats and dogs and horses. And they're old. I like it here."

Maddie almost saw the weight lifting from Ty as he closed his eyes briefly. She thought he was offering a prayer of thanksgiving. Not that anything was settled, but at least Darcy wouldn't be against living with her father.

"Besides, if I went to live with them, I'd miss the church picnic. And they probably wouldn't come here to visit and how could we sleep in the barn?"

"Good points," Ty said with a smile, which shone with love at his daughter.

Maddie hoped the judge could see the bond developing and give it the importance it deserved.

Monday morning, Maddie dropped Darcy at the church for the first day of Vacation Bible School. She chatted with some of the mothers dropping off their children and met one of the chairs from the picnic committee. Then she went to meet with Paul Linder at the Grasslands newspaper. She'd dressed in one of the few work outfits she'd brought, an emerald-green suit with a white silk blouse. It felt odd to be wearing a skirt again after so many weeks in jeans.

Paul came to greet her as soon as she was

announced. "Come on back here, the newspaper's hectic, but my office is an oasis."

It was. Maddie was delighted to see the big window in back overlooking a small flower garden in riotous color. The walls were a soothing pale blue, and the furniture was placed to take advantage of the view. His desk was stacked with papers and folders and newspapers, but the visitor's chair was free of any clutter.

"Sit and tell me a bit about yourself and what you're looking for in Grasslands," Paul said as he sat.

They chatted for several minutes. Maddie gave him a copy of her résumé and told him what she'd been doing since the layoff.

"Impressive job history," he remarked, perusing her résumé.

"Thanks. I know there are no magazines published around here, but I've learned a lot about project management, which I could use in any industry. I loved working at *Texas Today,* but you know the economic climate of publishing these days."

"I do, indeed. Fortunately, most of the subscribers of the newspaper are satisfied to get it as it's always been and not from a computer. But I can see one day that might change."

When Maddie was ready to leave, he promised to call around and see if he could discover anything suitable. She thanked him and left with a positive feeling that he might be able to help her.

Shortly after Maddie and Darcy had finished lunch that afternoon, the phone rang. It was Violet.

"There's a social worker here. She came to see Ty, so I've sent one of the men to find him. He's out somewhere on the range. Anyway, I'm sending her your way. She wants to see the house. Probably has to do with the hearing tomorrow."

"We're here, send her along." Maddie felt her heart drop. Glancing around she knew she couldn't clean up lunch before the social worker arrived. But at least the rest of the house was picked up and tidy.

"Wash your face and hands, we're going to have company in about two minutes," Maddie said to Darcy, dashing over to the sink to at least run water over the dishes.

Before Darcy came from the bathroom, the social worker was knocking on the door.

It was Mrs. Lucas, the one in charge of Darcy's case.

"Sorry to barge in like this," she said with a frown. "I know we make spot inspections, but this is a rush because of the hearing tomorrow. Is Mr. Garland around?"

"He'll be in as soon as one of the cowboys finds him. He's working on the range today. Come in. I'm Maddie Wallace, Darcy's nanny."

"So he did find someone, I'm so glad. I believe we spoke on the phone?"

"About Darcy's things, yes."

Darcy came down the hall, watching Mrs. Lucas warily.

"Hello, Darcy," she said with a warm smile.

"Hi." She went to stand next to Maddie, leaning against her slightly.

"She came to see your house and how you're doing," Maddie said lightly. "Want to show her your room while we wait for your daddy to join us?"

"Okay. It's down the hall."

Once the inspection was finished, Maddie offered Mrs. Lucas iced tea and they sat in the living room making small talk while they waited for Ty.

Maddie was dying to ask her about the visit, but knew the woman wouldn't be able to tell her anything. Still, it was like being on pins and needles. She hoped the report would be favorable.

Ty strode in a few minutes later.

"Mr. Garland," Mrs. Lucas said, smiling.

He did not return the smile, glancing at Maddie and Darcy.

"I think that's all I need from you," Mrs. Lucas said to Maddie. "Perhaps you and Darcy have some place you need to be?"

"We'll check on the horses, shall we?" Maddie asked, taking the hint. She wished she could stay with Ty, be there for support, but it was clear she wasn't wanted.

She positioned herself in the barn so she could see Mrs. Lucas's car. When the woman headed out, Maddie called Darcy and they headed back to Ty.

"Well?" she asked when she entered. He was on the sofa, legs stretched out in front of him.

"I have no idea how it went. I answered questions the best I could."

"Good, that's all you can do."

"Did she bring me any of my toys?" Darcy asked, going to sit by Ty.

He pulled her into his lap and hugged her. "I'm sorry, I forgot to ask her. We'll see her again." He looked at Maddie.

She hurt at the bleak expression in his eyes.

When they entered the courthouse in Floydada the next afternoon, Mrs. Lucas was in the hallway leading to the courtroom they'd been assigned. She smiled at them. "Early, that's good. The other party isn't here yet, but are expected."

Ty nodded.

Maddie wished she could say something to ease the tension, but the only thing that would work would be the judge granting custody to Ty.

She'd done as he'd asked and dressed as she often did at work in Fort Worth—a navy blue suit, white blouse and pearls. Her hair brushed her shoulders and she'd put on more makeup than she'd worn these last weeks. She knew she looked the part he wanted. Yet it felt strange, as if she were dressing up. To her surprise, she missed the jeans and boots.

He looked amazing in his Sunday attire. Strong and tall and resilient. Who could want a better man for a father?

Darcy had insisted on her boots, jeans and hat, and Ty had once again sided with her over Maddie's suggestion of something less in-your-face to her grandparents. The child was subdued and quiet, holding Ty's hand and looking around warily.

"Darcy, oh, thank goodness, there you are," a female voice called behind them.

They all turned. Maddie saw a tall woman with white hair, expertly styled, wearing an elegant dress of teal blue. Her eyes were focused on Darcy.

"Hi, Grandmama," Darcy said with a smile. She dropped Ty's hand and ran to greet the older woman. A moment later she skipped into the arms of an older man, obviously her grandfather. The older couple completely ignored Ty and Maddie, focused totally on their granddaughter.

"Oh, sweetie, I'm so sorry we weren't here when your mother died. You must have been so scared."

"Mrs. Lucas got me and then Daddy came and got me."

The older man looked over at Ty, his eyes hard. After a quick glance at Maddie and Mrs. Lucas, he turned back to Darcy.

"We're home now, sugar, and soon you'll be home with us."

"No, I want to stay with Daddy," Darcy said quickly. She looked at Ty. "I can stay with you, right, Daddy?"

He nodded.

Maddie reached out and clasped his hand for encouragement. He tightened his grip in acknowledgment.

The Parkers' attorney joined them. They

introduced him to Darcy just as Stephen Forester arrived. He greeted Ty and met Maddie and Mrs. Lucas. Then he turned and walked to the other attorney and introductions were made.

The bailiff came to the door. "Parker vs. Garland," he called.

"Why don't you wait here with me," Mrs. Lucas said, going over to Darcy. "We'll let the grownups talk and if they need us, they'll come get us."

Darcy looked at Ty. At his nod, she took Mrs. Lucas's hand and they walked to one of the wooden benches lining the wide hall.

The rest of them entered the courtroom, passing others on their way out. Stephen Forester directed Maddie where to sit in the audience portion, then he and Ty went to one of the tables in front of the judge. The Parkers and their attorney took the other table.

Maddie began to pray. She wanted so much for this to go right for Ty. Listening to the openings from each attorney, she wondered how the judge would rule. Of course she knew Ty, knew what kind of man he was, how he loved his daughter. But the Parkers also loved her, and had known her all her life.

At one point, Stephen mentioned a full-time nanny and asked Maddie to stand. The Parkers showed surprise when she did so.

To Maddie's astonishment, the judge asked her to the stand to answer some questions.

"How long have you know Ty Garland?" he asked.

"Almost two months. We met when I first came to visit my brother and sister at the Colby Ranch."

"Which explains why you look like Violet Colby," the judge said with a smile. "What's your assessment—as someone who has spent a lot of time with Darcy recently."

"She misses her mother. That was a huge blow. Even so, she seems to love living on the ranch. She's learned to ride, gone swimming in the river, has started church and is currently in Vacation Bible School, and is looking forward to attending Grasslands Elementary School in September. She and Ty are growing closer each day. He didn't know about her, you know."

"What?"

Briefly Maddie explained, which had the judge asking about that situation with the opposing attorney. His answer wasn't very helpful.

Once Maddie was excused, she hurried back to her seat hoping what she'd said would help.

Stephen gave her a wink as she passed and her heart lifted.

Chapter Ten

Without taking time to retire and consider things in private, the judge ruled the custody in favor of the father, Ty Garland. Ty sat stunned for a moment, then quickly offered a prayer of thanksgiving to the Lord before turning to shake Stephen's hand.

"Thanks, man. I couldn't have done it without you."

"Hey, that's what I'm here for. The change of venue and sudden opening in the judge's schedule worked for us as well." Stephen leaned closer. "Plus he knows the Colbys and their reputation of honesty and integrity. Go love that little girl and make her happy."

"I'll always do my best."

The Parkers were definitely angry. They

were conversing in a low voice with their attorney. Ty hesitated before leaving, but he wanted to get to Darcy, not make nice with her grandparents. Time for that later.

Maddie stood in the aisle as he joined her. She was smiling broadly. He hugged her exuberantly. "Let's go find our girl," he said.

Darcy was still sitting with Mrs. Lucas when Ty and Maddie burst into the hall.

"Are we going home now?" she asked.

"We sure are," Ty said, opening his arms and hugging her tightly when she ran to him.

Mrs. Lucas rose, a questioning smile on her face.

"He was awarded custody," Maddie explained.

"Good. She's happy there." She smiled gently. "There will be some rough times ahead, I'm sure, when she really misses her mother, but it was my recommendation she stay with him."

"Thank you for all you did."

The Parkers exited the courtroom and walked over to Ty.

"She's still our granddaughter," Aaron Parker insisted.

"Yes, she is. And she'll need you in her life."

The older man exhaled sharply. "But under your terms, I assume?"

"We'd like you to come visit us in the near future," Ty offered. "See where she's living now. See how well she's doing."

Arlene Parker touched the edge of Darcy's cowboy hat. "Your mother had one just like that," she said with a sad smile. "She loved cowboy stuff." She raised her eyes to Ty. "I believed she loved you for a time. The thought of giving up the excitement she so craved was more than she could deal with. Having Darcy changed that. She settled down a bit in Houston."

"I'm so sorry for her death and your loss. Darcy's loss." Ty didn't mention the fact no one had told him about Darcy. Everyone who needed to know that already did. At last he could forgive Brittany. Let go of the anger and heartache. He had been given a priceless gift and would rejoice in it, not dwell on the lateness of arrival.

Arlene nodded, touching Darcy again.

"You'll have to give us your phone number and email address," she choked off.

"I don't have a computer," Ty said. He gave her the phone number.

Maddie fished out a business card from her purse. "This email is mine. I'll bring my laptop to Ty's house and you can write or Skype Darcy whenever you wish."

"Once things get settled, you're welcome to come visit," Ty reiterated, trying to sound sincere.

"We're going to sleep in the barn when you do," Darcy piped up.

Ty almost groaned. That was not something he wanted her grandparents to dwell on.

"Camping out," Maddie murmured to defuse the anger she could see rising in Mr. Parker's face.

"How fun," Arlene said, although she obviously thought it was deplorable.

"Did you know Daddy has pictures of Mommy? When they were married and everything. I have them in my room," Darcy said.

Arlene's eyes filled with tears, and she looked at Ty. "Thank you for that."

"I loved Brittany. I'm sorry things didn't work out," he said softly.

Arlene smiled at Darcy. "Take good care of her."

"Always," Ty affirmed. "We'll be in touch. See about you coming to visit Darcy." Ty took Darcy's hand. Maddie reached for her other hand and they left the courthouse, conscious of the couple watching them walk away.

"You did good, cowboy," Maddie said softly, glancing at Ty.

"I thought I'd feel triumphant at the result, but they're hurting."

"You did the right thing, however."

Darcy looked from one to the other. "I'm glad I'm going back to the ranch. I want to go riding."

"You'll have plenty of time in the years ahead for riding," Ty said, giving her hand a squeeze. "You have your whole life ahead of you on the ranch."

The three of them were all quiet on the drive back to the Colby Ranch. Ty was relieved that he'd been granted custody. He offered another prayer to the Lord, and vowed to be better in trusting in Him. He glanced at Maddie from time to time. She gazed out the front windshield and he wondered what she was thinking.

At one point Darcy fell asleep leaning against Maddie. She put her arm around the child and drew her closer, but said nothing.

Ty began to worry as they neared the ranch. Had something happened that caused Maddie to be so silent?

"You okay?" he asked as they drove down Main Street in Grasslands.

"Fine. Grateful, thankful, happy for the ruling," she said. Glancing at him, she smiled. "As you must be."

"All that. And wondering a bit how I'll manage in the future. It's an awesome responsibility to raise a child."

"You're up to it. God will be with you every step."

He nodded. He wanted to suggest she be with him every step as well. The notion had been growing gradually. He reminded himself she was there temporarily. She did an amazing job with Darcy. She seemed to like being around him as well. He flat-out liked being with her.

Did she feel the same?

He thought back to Brittany. He had loved her, but had it been because of the good time they'd shared? Young, first love? Would it have stood the test of time?

He had not been a Christian back then. He would never party today like he had following the rodeo circuit. He doubted Brittany would even look at him today. Their love had been built on sand. He wanted a love built on a solid rock—like Christ said. A house built on solid rock would prevail. Especially if he and his wife put Christ in the center of their marriage.

Giving in to impulse, he turned the truck into the parking lot of Simmons Coffee Shop.

Maddie looked at him in surprise.

"This calls for a celebration, don't you think?"

"Yes, I do," she beamed.

They entered the coffee shop and took a booth near the front. As they opened the menus, Ty glanced at Maddie. She looked incredibly polished and sophisticated. She'd done as he'd asked for the hearing. It also reminded him of their obvious differences. She was city through and through. He was a rough cowboy, not happy unless he was working with horses and cattle. He could never fit in at Fort Worth.

"I'm having the pot roast. Rachel used to make the best pot roast. I have her recipe and should make that for us soon. Nothing like comfort food to celebrate with," she said, grinning at Ty and Darcy.

Catching his eye, her smile faltered. "What?"

"Nothing. That sounds good. I'm having the meatloaf."

"I want a hamburger," Darcy said. "With French fries and lots of ketchup."

Darcy chatted happily about her grandparents and her hope they could come visit soon. "But not until after Vacation Bible School and when real school starts. Unless they could come to the picnic. But I don't think they like picnics—we never go together on one.

Mommy took me to the park and we had picnics."

"And now you go with your dad and me," Maddie said affectionately.

Ty studied the table as he let the conversation swirl around him. They had done several things as a family. Maddie seemed happy to join in. And Darcy clearly adored her. Yet he couldn't help feel the gulf between their lifestyles. If they wanted a future together, something would have to give. He hadn't a clue if she was thinking along the same lines as he was. And without something concrete to offer, it was a moot point to bring it up.

She laughed and he looked at her. She was so beautiful—especially when she laughed. If nothing else, he'd keep moments like these in his memory forever.

Saturday morning dawned clear and warm. Maddie was up early, checking on all the last-minute details for the picnic. Ty and Darcy were picking her up at nine and she wanted everything to be ready.

Lupita and Violet had helped her pull out all

the tables, chairs, fly covers and other items Belle usually saw to at the annual event each year. Ty had loaded everything in his truck. There remained only the side dishes they were contributing. Lupita had made a huge bowl of potato salad. The bowl nestled in a larger bowl of ice to keep it cold until eaten. Violet had baked dozens of rolls and made two kinds of butter—savory and sweet—to go with them. Everyone said Maddie was excused from bringing a side dish since she was doing all the coordinating—and Lupita made enough for four contributions.

When the horn sounded at nine, Maddie grabbed her folder and dashed out.

"Good morning," she said breathlessly when she climbed into the cab of the truck.

"Good morning," Ty and Darcy responded.

"I can't wait for the picnic! I have my swimsuit on under my clothes and we brought towels and sunscreen," the little girl said excitedly.

"But when you're not swimming, keep that hat on," her father reminded her.

"Okay."

"All set?" Ty asked Maddie.

"Yes—or as ready as I can be."

They were not the first to arrive at Fraser's Lake. Pastor Jeb and Sadie were already there, as well as several others already helping to set up. Sadie was showing people where to put the food. Jeb was firing up the large brick barbecue pit.

Ty and Darcy helped Maddie unload all the items from the back. The next hour was spent setting up tables, spreading disposable tablecloths on all the picnic tables, dusting off benches, setting up chairs and hauling floats and inner tubes to the water's edge.

"You don't go swimming until there is an adult to watch you," Ty admonished.

"I won't. When will others be here?" Darcy asked, dancing with excitement.

No sooner had she spoken than two more cars pulled into the parking area. A moment later, a truck. From then on it was a steady stream of families arriving.

Darcy went to play with some of her new friends from Vacation Bible School and one mother volunteered to watch the kids if they wanted to swim. That set off a rush to the water.

Maddie did a final check with the committee chairs and then turned the folder over to Sadie for use next year.

"You've done a great job," Sadie remarked, looking at all the families enjoying themselves.

"Only a bit of organization—everyone was already set. I appreciate the chance to get to know so many people in a short time."

"Umm," Sadie said, glancing across the space where Jeb stood laughing with several other men as they hovered around the barbecue.

"It wasn't hard," Maddie repeated. "Next year you can handle it fine, and if I'm still here, I'll help."

"If I'm still here…" Sadie murmured.

"Don't you like Grasslands?" Maddie asked, startled by the comment.

"This is the happiest I've ever been, I think," Sadie said. She smiled wryly at Maddie and then headed for the heavily laden table and the newcomers, who were bringing even more.

"You did as good a job as Mom would have," Violet said, coming to stand by her twin. "People will think we are deliberately dressing like twins if we both keep wearing yellow blouses."

Maddie grinned. "I know, but it's my favorite color. I wanted to look nice when meeting so many people. Oh, and I forgot to tell you last night. Paul Linden left a message for me on my cell—he has a potential job I might be interested in."

"Fabulous! And you are only telling me now?"

"With getting everything ready for the picnic, it went out of my head."

"He'll be here today, find out what he has in mind," Violet instructed.

"Business with pleasure?" Maddie asked doubtfully.

"Of course. He'll probably seek you out, but if he doesn't, you find him."

The day passed in a whirl. Maddie was introduced to the entire town, she was sure. Some faces she recognized from church. Others she'd met in the weeks she'd lived here.

She knew it would take some time to associate children with parents, husbands with wives, and others. But she enjoyed meeting everyone.

After lunch was over, the children and adults so inclined splashed in the water. Others spread blankets in the shade or had brought chairs. Groups expanded and contracted as people visited.

"Having fun?" Ty asked at one point. She hadn't had a chance to talk to him since they'd arrived early that morning.

"I am," she said with a happy sigh. "However, I'll be glad when we leave. I'm getting smiler's cramp."

"What?"

"I've smiled so much today my cheeks ache."

"Want to take off?"

"Can we do that? I mean, I was in charge of this so should I stay until the end?"

"Don't see why. Your clean-up committee will make sure the grounds are spotless before they leave. Some families have already left. If we can corral Darcy, we can head back."

"Oh, she's having so much fun. We can wait."

"Or maybe Violet and Landon will bring her home," he suggested.

Maddie smiled again, then groaned and put both hands to her cheeks as the muscles protested. "Great idea."

Ty smiled into her eyes. "You go get in the truck, so no one catches you to hold us up. I'll find Violet and ask."

In less than ten minutes, they pulled out of the parking area and headed for the ranch. Maddie felt comfortably tired. She'd pulled it off, but it was no great feat. She'd had the help of so many members of Grasslands Community Church. What a great family of Christians.

"Tired?"

"A bit."

"I'll drop you at the main house when we arrive," he said.

"Okay." She looked at him and felt her heart rate increase. He'd been in the thick of things today, helping with the barbecuing, watching out for one of the elderly men who found the uneven ground difficult to walk on. She hadn't been able to eat with him and Darcy, but noticed he'd had others to spend the time with.

"I think I have a job offer," she said, watching for his initial reaction.

"Where?" he asked.

His hands tightened on the steering wheel and he kept his eyes on the road ahead. Interesting.

"Here in Grasslands, actually. Paul Linden is expanding the newspaper slightly and wants a project manager. With my experience at the magazine, which he took the time to find out, he says I'll be perfect. It doesn't pay as much as my job in Fort Worth, but I don't figure my expenses will be as high here, either."

Ty flicked her a glance. "So you're staying."

She nodded.

"I told him I could spend time evenings learning the job if he liked, but nothing during the day until school starts. He's okay with that." She smiled. "Actually, I'm excited. I think it'll be a great opportunity. And Violet said I should plan to live here at least until I get back on my feet. I still have to pay rent in Fort Worth until the lease expires."

"Good," Ty said.

And that was all.

Maddie was a little disappointed. She had hoped for a more enthusiastic response.

"So I can still spend time with you and Darcy," she reassured him.

"She'll like that."

Would he?

Maddie waited, but he didn't say anything more. He couldn't be still hung up on her being from Fort Worth. How to convince him once and for all that she was nothing like Brittany? To get him to change his mind and open it up for whatever the Lord had in store for him.

And for her.

He stopped in front of the main house. "You did an awesome job with the picnic, especially coming in at the last minute like that," Ty said as he half turned toward her.

"I didn't do much. Next year Sadie will be able to handle it. I think she could have this year, but she seemed so hesitant. I'm not sure why. In fact, today she even said something about possibly not being here next year. Maybe Grasslands isn't for her. But it is for me!" There, how blatant could she make it?

"Rest up, you deserve it. We'll see you in the morning?"

"Of course."

Maddie went straight inside. It wasn't that hard a day, the most difficult part had been meeting so many new people and trying to remember names and faces. Now that she was back at the ranch, however, she relished the chance to do nothing.

Rejuvenated a short time later, she gave in to an impulse and drove to Ranchland Manor to see Belle.

The room was bright and airy, in contrast to the hospital-like setting with tubes and machines and all that surrounded Belle.

"Hi," Maddie said, pulling a chair close to the bed. She took Belle's hand and squeezed it gently. "It's Maddie. I came to tell you about the picnic. You were very much missed. So many people said to tell you hi. I'll try to remember them all. And everyone at the church is praying for you. Please wake up soon."

There was no response.

"So first Pastor Jeb opened the picnic with prayer. The kids had a ball in the lake and there were quite a few moms and dads in there as well." She related as much as she could about the day, wishing Belle could have been there. Wishing she knew if Belle was processing any of her conversation.

"I have a job offer—here in Grasslands. I'll get to spend more time with Violet and Jack and be here when you wake up. We're still trying to reach Dad, but no luck there."

She gazed out the window at the large trees for a few seconds.

"Then there's Ty Garland." She waited a moment. But there was no reaction from Belle. "I think I'm in love with him. He's a hard man to read. And nothing like Landon. Did you know I was engaged to him briefly? But that wasn't a fit. I think with Ty it could be." She poured out her feelings for Ty, for the hard breaks he'd had in life, and the re-sounding triumph of his getting custody of his daughter. She was learning patience throughout this summer and she hoped if it was meant to be that she'd be patient enough for Ty to find out what he wanted. She hoped it would be her.

When she finished, she sat quietly beside the woman who had given her birth and then relinquished her. What had happened? Would they ever know for certain?

When Maddie heard the dinner carts in the hall, she stood. "I'm going now. They are serving dinner to the other patients and will be in soon to check on you. Next year I hope you're back in charge of the church picnic. Wake up, please. We want you back with us in the worst way."

She gave Belle a kiss on her cheek and left.

It felt right to bring Belle up to date on her situation. She was her mother, of that there was no doubt. Maybe if she awoke, she and Maddie could build a relationship as strong as she had with Violet.

Pulling out her cell, she gave Rachel a call and brought her up to date. As she'd told

Darcy, a person could have more than one mother. She was lucky, she had three.

When Maddie returned to the ranch, Landon's car still hadn't returned. The picnic was going longer than she expected. She imagined the kids were most reluctant to stop playing in the lake.

She went to Ty's house, but a quick knock produced no response. She headed to the barn.

He was in the tack room, working on some reins.

"Working on Saturday?" she said, leaning against the doorjamb.

He looked up, studying her for a moment. "Work never ends around a ranch."

"Ummm. Turns out I wasn't as tired as I thought I was. I went to see Belle. To tell her I'm staying here."

"Still the same?"

She nodded sadly. "It's ironic, I found her but she doesn't know that. I wonder if she's missed me all these years."

"I'm certain she has," Ty said, continuing to rub the saddle soap into the leather.

"No one else is back from the picnic. I didn't think it would go that long."

"It didn't. Violet called and she and Landon took Darcy to town. They're going to eat there and have ice cream, then come home."

"Oh. Want me to fix us dinner?"

"No need. This is your day off."

"I have to eat. We might as well eat together. You know, I've been thinking. Once school starts, I could take Darcy in every day when I go in for work. I don't think I'll be getting off when she gets out of school, but if you find someone in town to watch her after school, I could bring her home when I return."

"Until you get a place in town," he said.

"Which could be months down the road."

His jaw stiffened. "You don't have to do that," he said.

She grew exasperated. "I'm offering because I want to. I know I don't have to. That way, I'd still see her every day."

"And that's important?"

She looked around the tack room, unsure of how to answer that. She wanted to be completely honest with him, but did he really want to hear the truth?

"Maddie?" he said, looking concerned.

She met his gaze.

"It's important to me. I love your daughter," she blurted out.

He stared at her for a long moment, then, deliberately holding her gaze, put down the reins and stood. In three steps he was right in front of her.

"She loves you, too. But what if you leave? Won't that be almost as hurtful for her as her mother's death?"

"You're the only one who keeps thinking I'm leaving. I don't know how to change your mind. You'll just have to accept it on faith. I just found half my family. I love living here in Grasslands. I'm getting a new job. Why would I leave?"

There was another—stronger—reason, but she couldn't tell him.

He stared at her for a long moment. Maddie could almost see the battle going on in his mind.

He smiled at her, and her heart flip-flopped.

"I don't want you to leave. You know some- times when you want something so badly it hurts, you're afraid to go after it in case it vanishes?"

She frowned. "I think I know what you're talking about."

"That's how I feel about you."

She knew the surprise she felt showed on her face. "What?"

"I want you to stay so badly I can almost taste it. Once before I was happy, and it was snatched away. I'm afraid to reach out for it again. The disappointment is hard to take. It's easier to just go with the flow and not yearn for anything."

She nodded to encourage him to keep talk- ing. She wasn't sure—was he really talking about her?

"You know I didn't exactly welcome you with open arms when you arrived on the ranch. Even when Violet suggested you watch Darcy, I wasn't sure how things would work out. You are special, Maddie, in ways I never expected. I like to watch the delight in your eyes when something catches your fancy. I love your laughter—it's contagious and makes everyone around you feel happier. I'm in awe of how you relate to Darcy. I especially like it when you smile at me as if we are the only two people on the earth."

"I don't know what to say." Which was true. The way her heart was pounding, she wasn't sure she could talk. Hope blossomed deep inside. Her eyes never left his.

He reached out and tucked a strand of hair behind her ear as if he couldn't not make some kind of connection between them.

"I have a lot of baggage coming with me, and an eight-year-old girl. But if I ask you a question, will you answer honestly?" he said.

"I'm always honest," she said.

"How do you feel about me?"

That was throwing a curveball at her. Her heart rate increased, her palms grew damp. Dare she confess that she loved him and wanted nothing more than to get to know him better, to spend the days ahead with him and Darcy? Or was he merely asking if she liked working for him?

"It shouldn't be that hard," he said.

She could see the barriers building. Trusting in her heart, she smiled.

"I love you, Ty. More than I ever thought possible."

"Yeehaw!" he yelled, picking her up and spinning them both around and around.

He set her on her feet and cupped her face in his hands, kissing her soundly on the lips.

"I love you, Maddie Wallace. I fought against it, tried to put you in the same box Brittany came from. Even if you were like that, I would still want to tie my life with yours." He released a ragged breath. "If you can't stay in Grasslands, we'll find a place to suit us both. But no matter what, I want you to marry me. If we live here on the ranch all the better and you can be near your sister and brother. Be a mother to my daughter, and a wife to me. What do you say?"

Happiness broke like a wave through her. "I say yes!" She flung her arms around his neck and he caught her close, hugging her against him. "I love you, so much. Despite your incorrigible attitude, which drives me *crazy* sometimes. I would love to be your wife. To learn more about ranching, watch Darcy grow up. This place is perfect for us. Yes, yes, yes!"

He swept her into his arms and kissed her. She kissed him back with all the love in her heart.

She couldn't believe he'd asked her. She'd hoped he was growing fond of her, but this was beyond anything she expected after knowing him for only a few weeks.

He ended the kiss, resting his forehead against hers. "I've been praying about this for a week or longer, and praying for nerve to ask. If you wanted to return to Fort Worth, I'd see if I could get a job there. There are ranches in the area, stockyards that need cowhands."

"Our life here is perfect. There's nothing in Fort Worth to hold me there. I have it all here—with you. You and Darcy."

"Then how soon will you marry me? I can't wait to have you with me, sharing meals, planning for the future. Learning how to be a rancher's wife."

"Oh. Oh, I don't know." Uncertainty clouded her features. "I need to find my dad. I need to tell my brothers—all three of them. And, would you mind if we wait until we know if Belle's going to wake up? I'm not quite ready to give up on the dream of having both my parents at my wedding."

"Whatever you want. I want you to be happy, Maddie."

"I shall be, every day I spend with you and Darcy. And maybe with some kids of our own? You do know twins run in my family."

He smiled down at her. "So we get a bigger house, maybe even a spread of our own one day. I never thought I'd marry again. But I didn't plan to fall in love again, either. But I did." He kissed her softly. "Now I can't wait until you're my wife."

"Me, too. In the meantime, I'll still be fixing breakfast and dinner for the three of us—except for the days we eat with Violet and Jack. Oh, won't they be surprised. Both of us engaged in less than three months of meeting each other." Her eyes sparkled with joy. "I can't wait to tell her. And Darcy. You think she'll be happy with the news?"

"She'll be thrilled. I think she already thinks of you as her second mom. Whatever the future holds, we'll face it together—in love and faith."

"Yes, in faith and love."

He kissed her again, sealing the vow, the promise for the future.

When Landon and Violet returned home with Darcy, Ty and Maddie hurried to the main house to share their news. Jack was there, heading out back to the house he was renovating. He'd skipped the picnic, staying close to the house during the day in case someone was needed with the others at the church event.

"Hi, Jack," Maddie greeted him. "Don't leave just yet—we have news," she said as he almost passed them in the doorway.

"You've heard from Brian?" he asked, looking between Ty and Maddie.

"No."

"What's up?" Violet asked, as she and Landon joined them in the entryway. "You heard from your dad?"

Maddie shook her head, then burst out, "Ty and I are engaged!"

Violet squealed and rushed to hug Maddie.

Landon smiled and shook hands with Ty. "You're getting a gem."

"I know."

"Good grief, is everyone going crazy?" Jack growled. "If this love stuff is in the water, I'm drinking milk from now on." He rammed his hat onto his head and strode out.

"I'm so happy for you both," Violet said, hugging Maddie and smiling at Ty. "Don't mind Mr. Grouch. He's got a lot on his plate with Mom, and meeting you and learning about Grayson. Plus," she lowered her voice and said, "he lost the woman he loved last year. I think it's all getting to be too much for him."

"What's *engaged?*" Darcy asked, coming into the entry.

"It means when Belle's awake and able to attend, Maddie's marrying me," Ty said.

"She's going to be my new mom?" Darcy asked, her eyes lighting up.

"Yes, and my wife," Ty said, his gaze seeking Maddie's.

"Forever," she said, reaching out for his hand, love shining from her eyes.

He drew her in with one arm and reached down to scoop Darcy up in his other arm. Hugging them both, he nodded. "Forever."

* * * * *

Dear Reader,

Welcome to Grasslands, Texas. Join Maddie Wallace as she continues to learn more about her newly discovered twin, Violet Colby, while visiting the Colby Ranch. Unanswered questions abound as Maddie tries to learn as much as she can about what happened when they were babies and why neither had known the other existed until a month ago.

Had it been the Lord's will she was laid off just when she discovered her twin so she was able to visit for an extended period of time? Maddie believes so. When a job opens as nanny for the ranch foreman, she knows the Lord is leading her to stay. Yet frustrations occur daily as they seek answers to the riddle of their past.

I love Texas, the wide-open spaces and the endless blue skies. Trying to imagine how a city girl like Maddie would adjust to life on a ranch was such fun, and I hope you'll enjoy finding out how Maddie makes a special place for herself at the ranch, and in the heart of a cowboy who had been burned badly by love in the past. The Lord's hand is evident in all they do, and in the love they find.

Happy reading,

Barbara McMahon

Questions for Discussion

1. In the beginning of the book, Maddie is starting a new job. She has little or no experience in taking care of a child. Do her thoughts on taking over the responsibility reflect what you would have thought? How would your ideas on this new job match or not match Maddie's?

2. The reason Maddie is on the ranch is due to recently discovering she has a twin sister and older brother she never knew. She's visiting the ranch to get to know them. How would you feel if suddenly you discovered a sibling you never knew about? Would you want them to come to your place to learn more about you, or go to theirs to learn more about them?

3. How would you view a totally different lifestyle such as Maddie is seeing? Plunge right in to embrace the best features, or rail against the differences and long to return to home?

4. Ty Garland discovered he has an eight-year-old daughter only recently, when her mother died. How would you respond to a similar situation? Do you think his handling of the situation is best? Or should he have found a different way?

5. Darcy is obviously hurting from her mother's death. How would you have suggested Maddie deal with that situation? Do you think at age eight talking about it more would help? Did pictures of her mother help? Do you think in addition to everything else, she missed her things?

6. One Sunday Ty takes Darcy on a picnic and includes Maddie. Do you think it was a good idea to have the three of them do things together? Did that help Darcy, or hinder the bonding between her and her newly found father?

7. Maddie is constantly trying to reach her father to ask him about Violet and Jack. What would you do that Maddie didn't do to try to reach him? Would you be as

anxious to learn more about what split the family apart, or take it on faith all would be revealed in due time?

8. Maddie spends more time with Violet than with Jack, yet when they decided to visit Fort Worth to check out their former home, Jack is right there with them. Does this show he's interested in learning more about the past, or just going along out of family solidarity? Do you think his taking off to work on the old house is running away, or really giving him a chance to regroup and think things through?

9. Maddie is asked to take over the coordination of the church picnic. Belle was originally in charge. Do you think she was best suited for this, or should another member of the congregation have stepped up? Would you volunteer for a project like this to fit in better and get to know more people, or wait until you'd been in town longer?

10. Maddie appears upbeat and confident about the future, though she is out of work

and not even sure where she wants to live. This is a testament to her faith. How would you react to a similar situation of being out of work and getting to decide to stay in your hometown, or try something new in a new town?

11. How would you feel if after twenty-five years you discovered the woman you always thought was your mother was not in fact your mother? Would you have visited Belle as often as Maddie did and talk about what you're doing? Would you become discouraged about whether she'd ever recover? What other things might you do to discover more about this newly found mother?

12. Knowing your father lied to you all your life, how would you view him at this point? Would you be anxious to learn the truth of the situation, or angry at him and wanting to put some distance between you and him? How does forgiveness factor in?

13. How did you feel when you learned about Darcy's grandparents wanting to have her

live with them? Would that be a better choice—living with people she'd known all her life, or would staying with her father be the better choice? Do you feel Darcy's new allegiance is appropriate, or did you feel she should have gone with her grandparents?

14. Ty's faith is strengthened as the story progresses. Have you found a time when adversity or hard times strengthened your own walk in faith? What was the outcome?

15. What do you think Maddie and Violet should have done further to discover who is sending them the Bibles? What would you do if you received a gift of a Bible with a cryptic note?